AUG 0 9

BUZZ BEAKER
vs
Dracula

STONE ARCH BOOKS
www.stonearchbooks.com

Graphic Sparks are published by Stone Arch Books
151 Good Counsel Drive, P.O. Box 669
Mankato, Minnesota 56002
www.stonearchbooks.com

Library of Congress Cataloging-in-Publication Data
Nickel, Scott.
Buzz Beaker vs Dracula: A Buzz Beaker Brainstorm / by Scott Nickel; illustrated by Andy J. Smith.
p. cm. — (Graphic Sparks. A Buzz Beaker Brainstorm)
ISBN 978-1-4342-1191-0 (library binding)
ISBN 978-1-4342-1388-4 (pbk.)
1. Graphic novels. [1. Graphic novels. 2. Vampires—Fiction.] I. Smith, Andy J., 1975– ill. II. Title.
PZ7.7.N53Buz 2009
741.5'973—dc22 2008032058

Summary: Sure, Dracula can live forever, but he really just wants to hit the beach! To catch some waves, the blood-sucking bat will need a little help. That's why he's captured the brainy Buzz Beaker. Now, this wacky whiz kid must turn the Lord of the Vampires into the King of the Beach, or he could be the monster's next meal.

Creative Director: Heather Kindseth
Graphic Designer: Emily Harris

1 2 3 4 5 6 14 13 12 11 10 09

Printed in the United States of America

BUZZ BEAKER
vs
Dracula

by Scott Nickel

illustrated by Andy J. Smith

Cast of Characters

Buzz Beaker

Dracula

The Bloodsuckers

Fangz

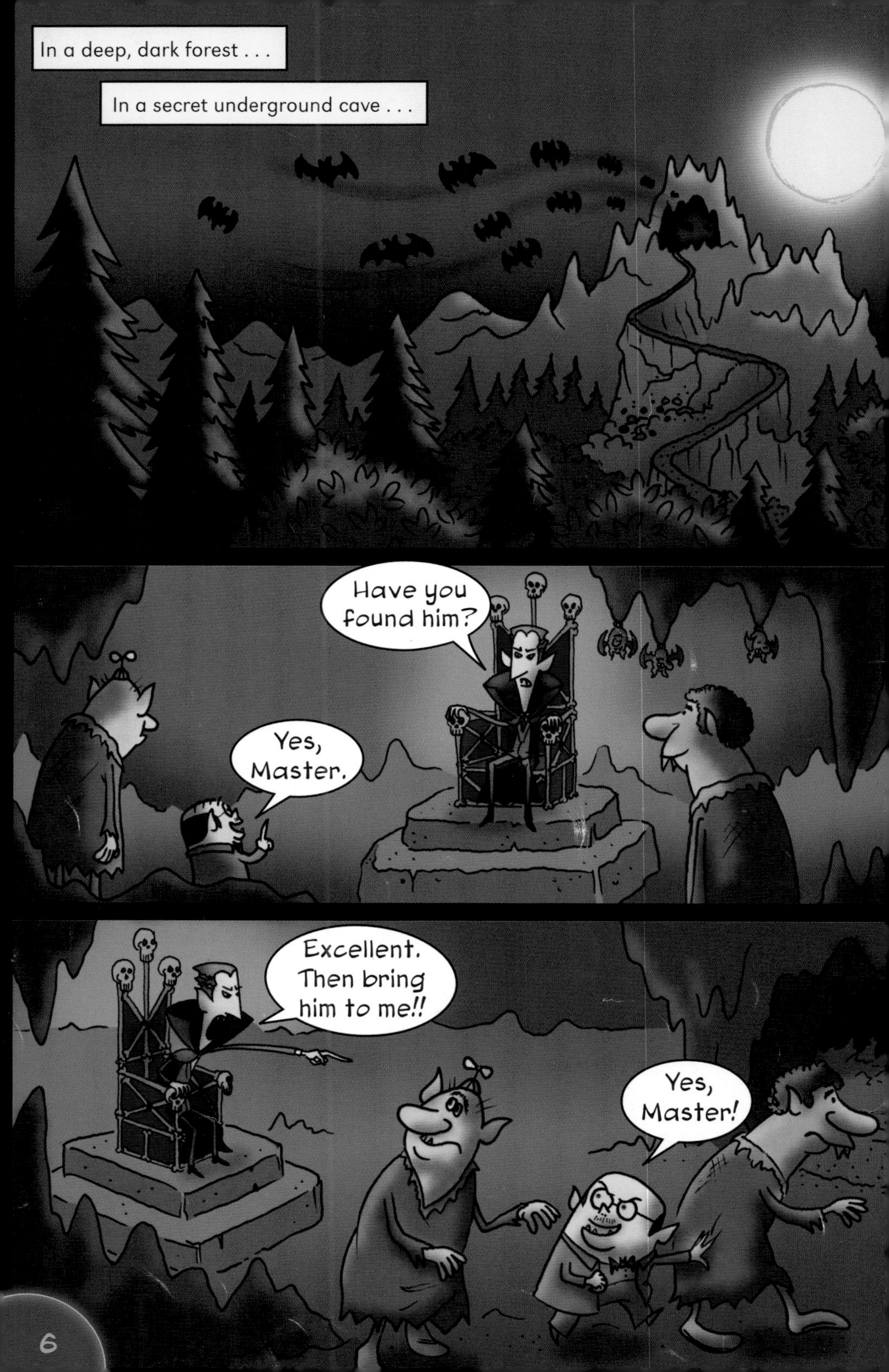

In a deep, dark forest . . .
In a secret underground cave . . .
Have you found him?
Yes, Master.
Excellent. Then bring him to me!!
Yes, Master!

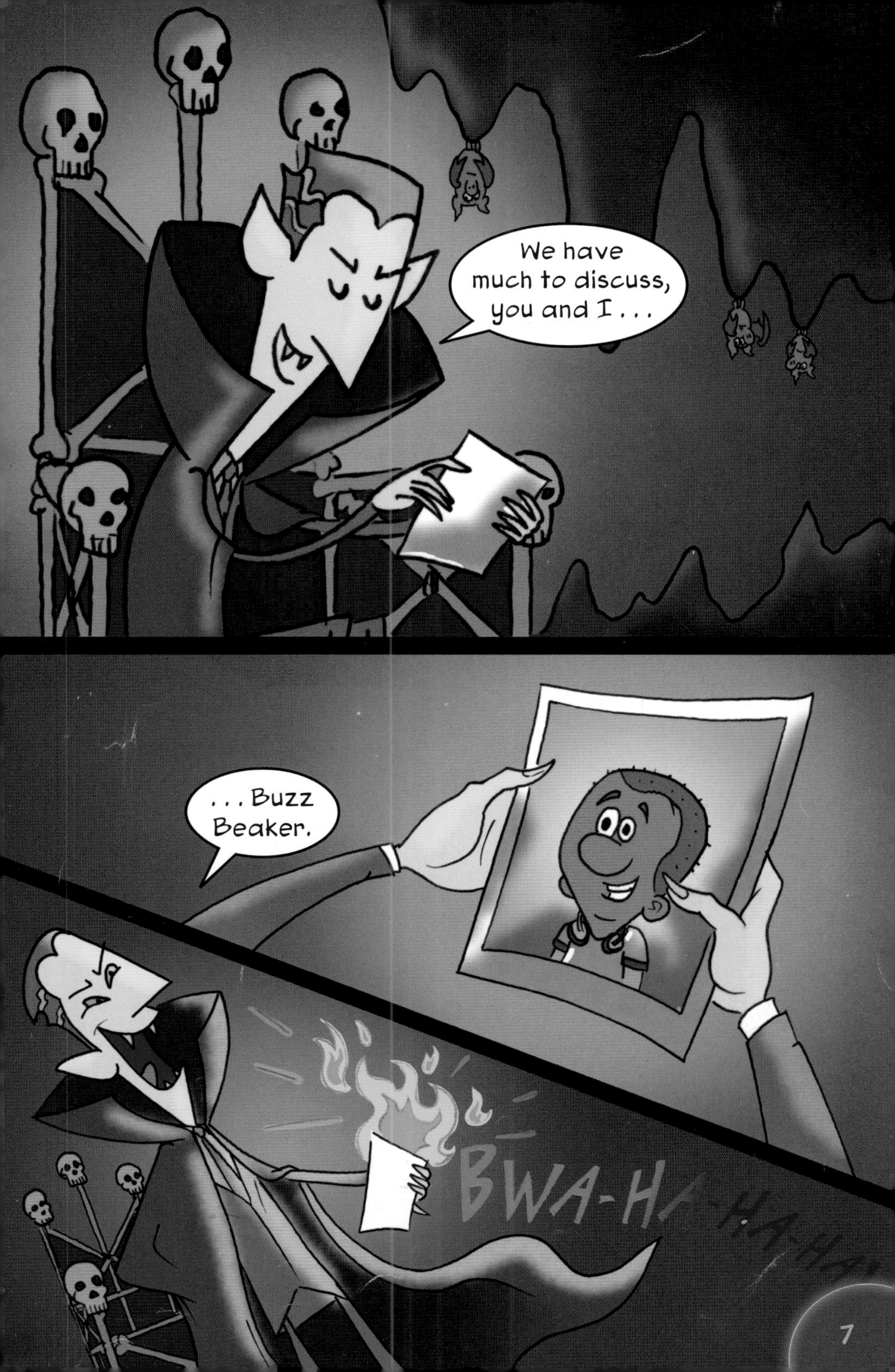

We have much to discuss, you and I . . .
. . . Buzz Beaker.
BWA-HA-HA-HA!

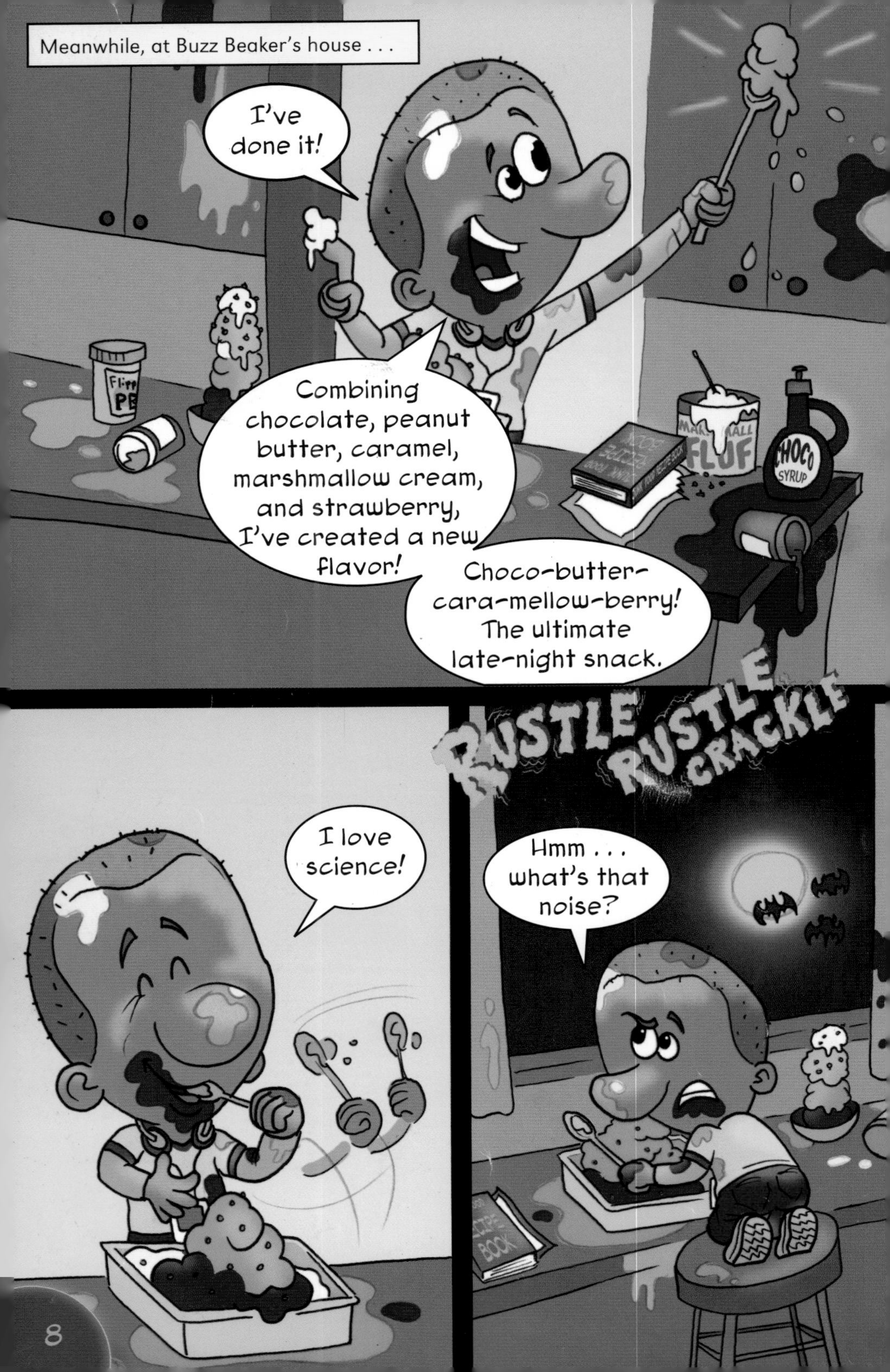
Meanwhile, at Buzz Beaker's house . . .
I've done it!
Combining chocolate, peanut butter, caramel, marshmallow cream, and strawberry, I've created a new flavor!
Choco-butter-cara-mellow-berry! The ultimate late-night snack.
CHOCO SYRUP
I love science!
RUSTLE RUSTLE CRACKLE
Hmm . . . what's that noise?

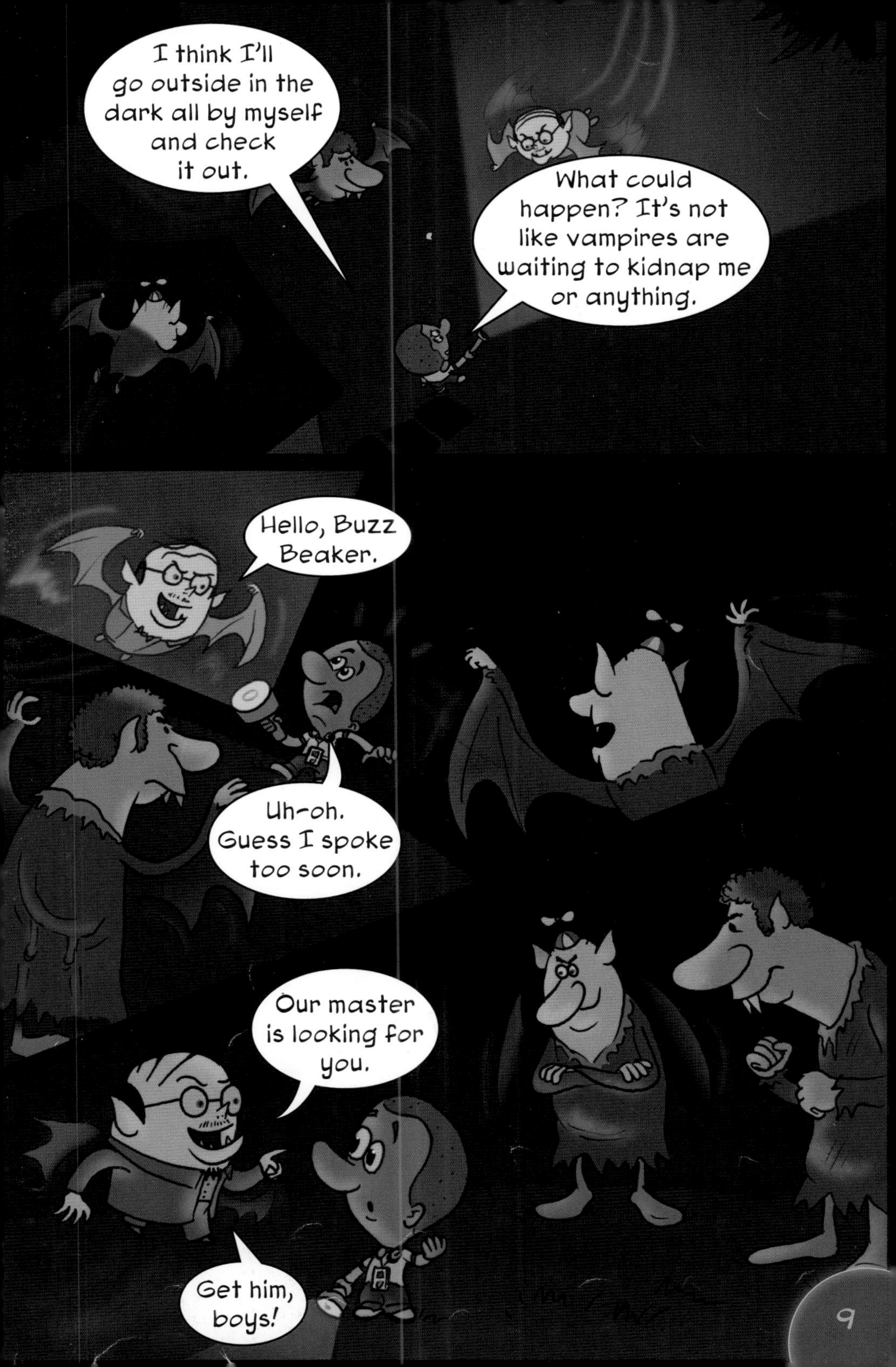
I think I'll go outside in the dark all by myself and check it out.
What could happen? It's not like vampires are waiting to kidnap me or anything.
Hello, Buzz Beaker.
Uh-oh. Guess I spoke too soon.
Our master is looking for you.
Get him, boys!

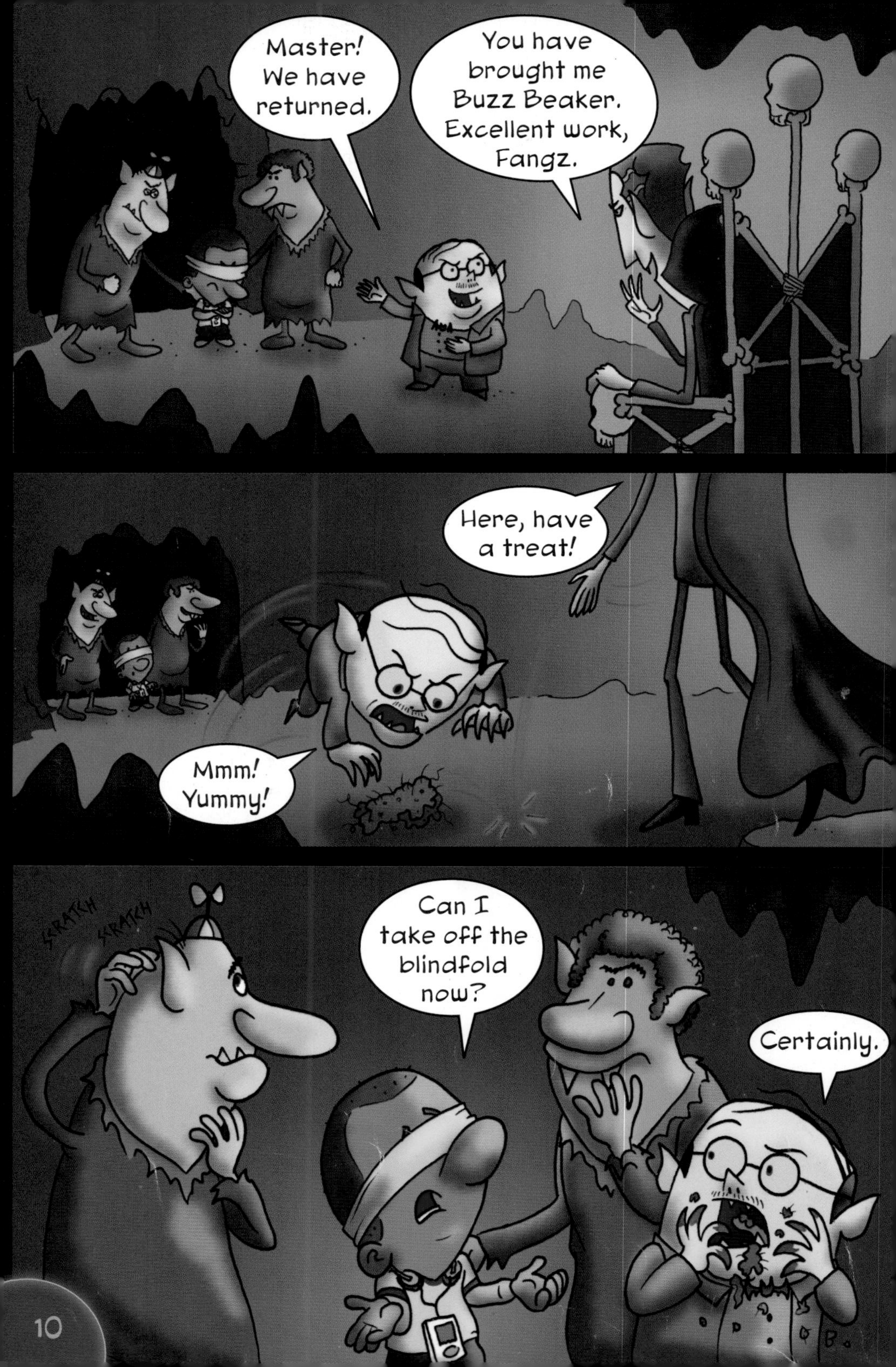
Master! We have returned.
You have brought me Buzz Beaker. Excellent work, Fangz.
Here, have a treat!
Mmm! Yummy!
SCRATCH SCRATCH
Can I take off the blindfold now?
Certainly.

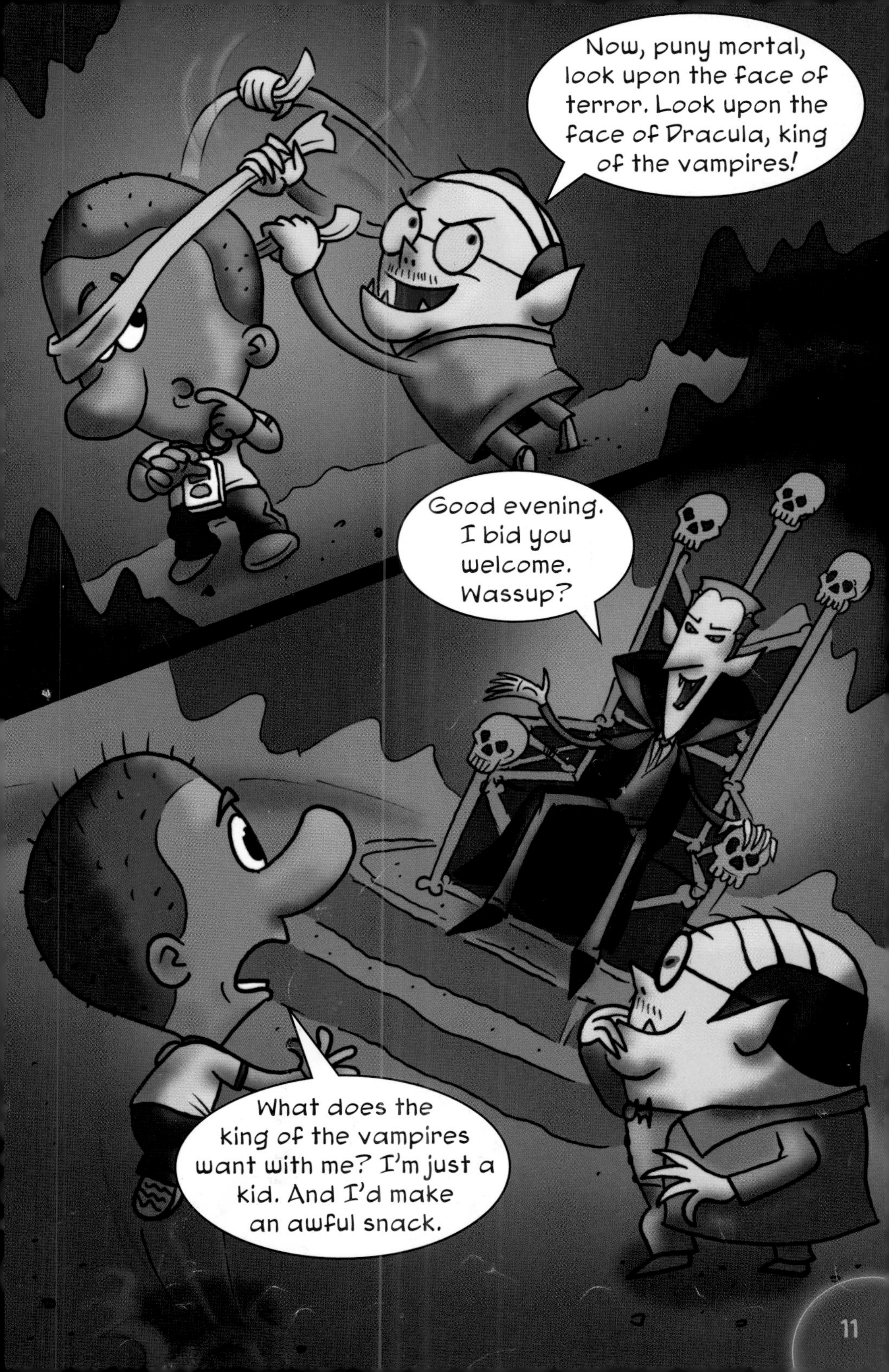
Now, puny mortal, look upon the face of terror. Look upon the face of Dracula, king of the vampires!
Good evening. I bid you welcome. Wassup?
What does the king of the vampires want with me? I'm just a kid. And I'd make an awful snack.

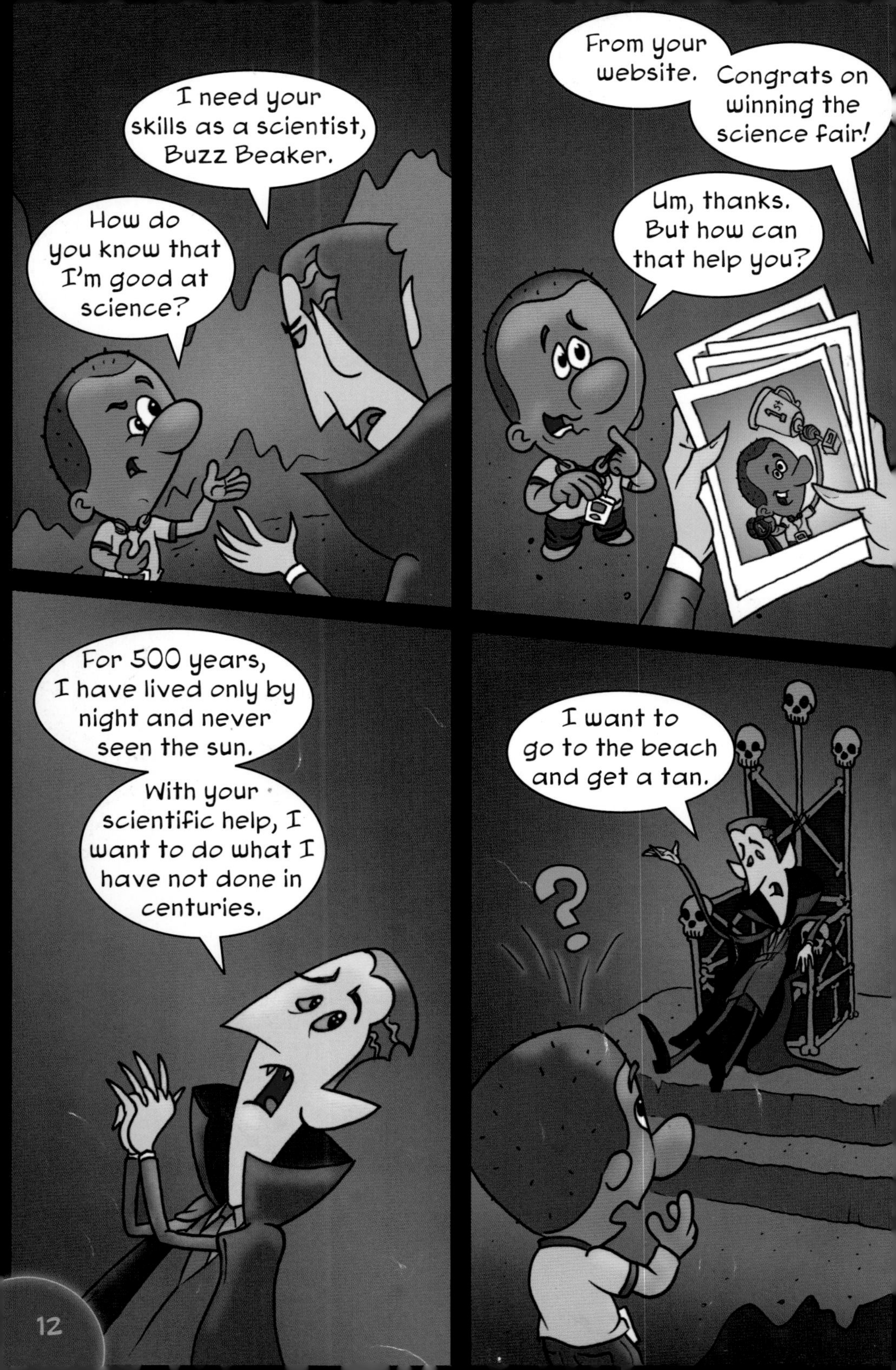
I need your skills as a scientist, Buzz Beaker.
How do you know that I'm good at science?
From your website.
Congrats on winning the science fair!
Um, thanks. But how can that help you?
For 500 years, I have lived only by night and never seen the sun.
With your scientific help, I want to do what I have not done in centuries.
I want to go to the beach and get a tan.
?

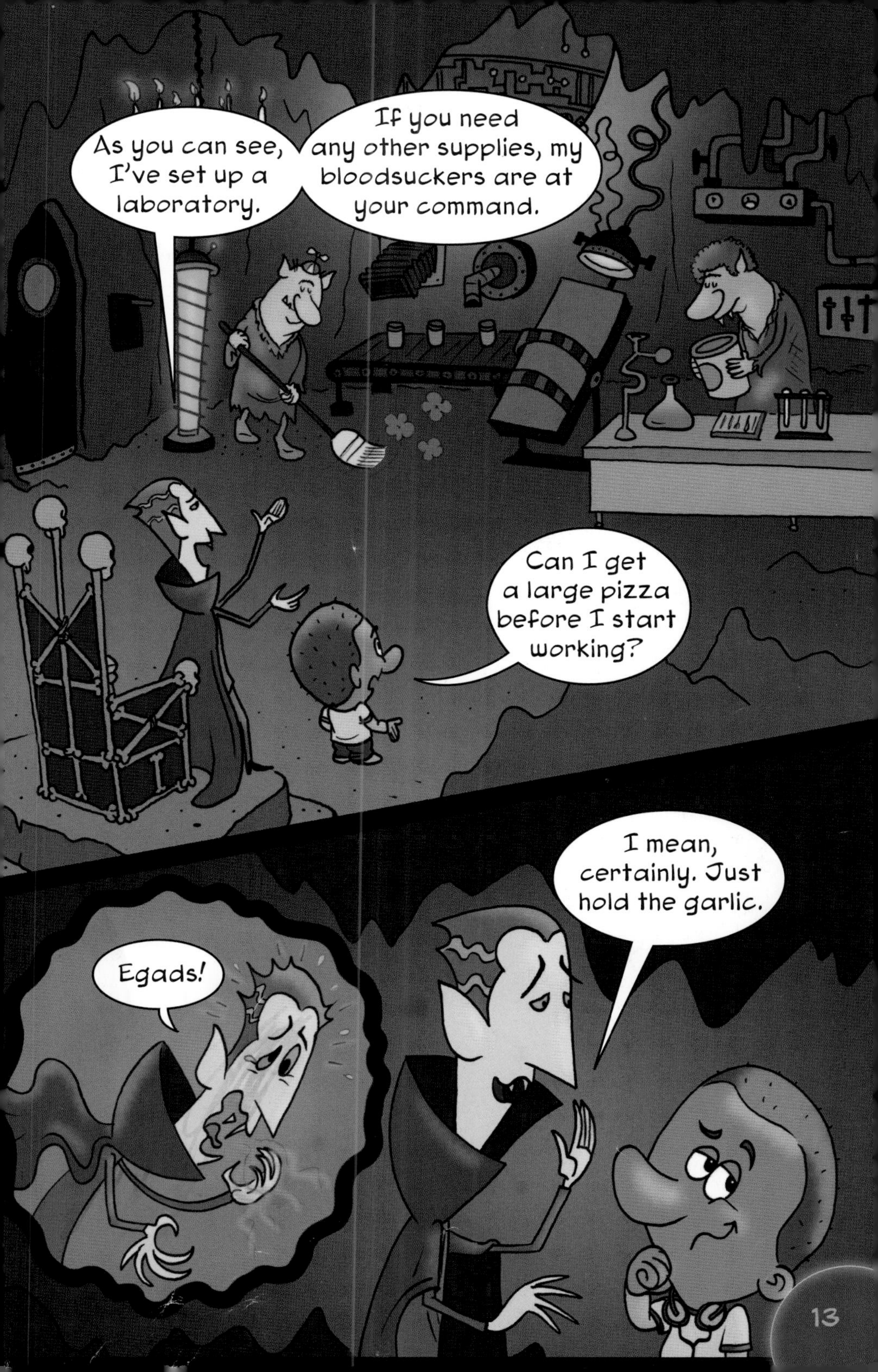
As you can see, I've set up a laboratory.
If you need any other supplies, my bloodsuckers are at your command.
Can I get a large pizza before I start working?
I mean, certainly. Just hold the garlic.
Egads!

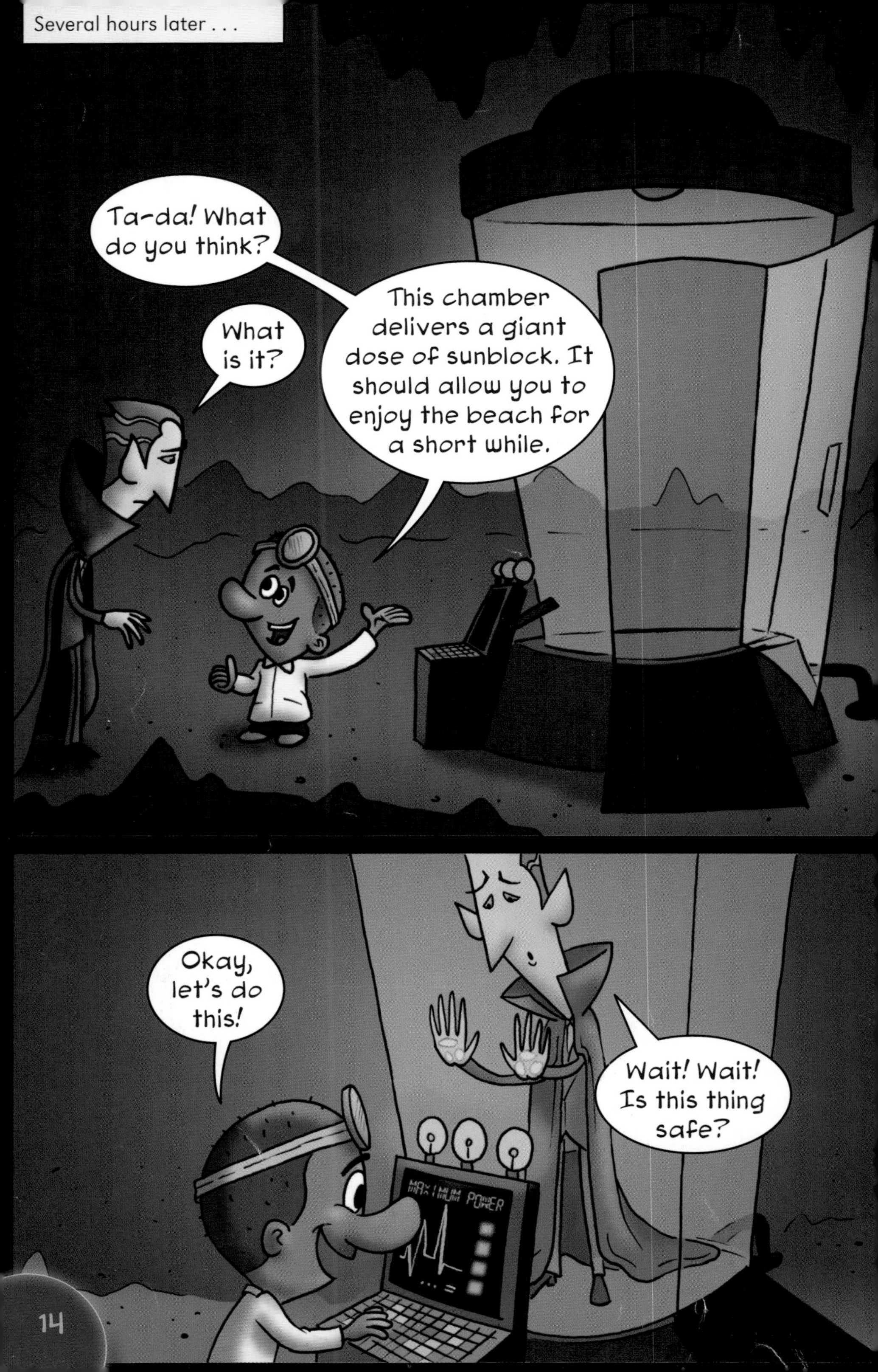
Several hours later . . .
Ta-da! What do you think?
What is it?
This chamber delivers a giant dose of sunblock. It should allow you to enjoy the beach for a short while.
Okay, let's do this!
Wait! Wait! Is this thing safe?
MAXIMUM POWER

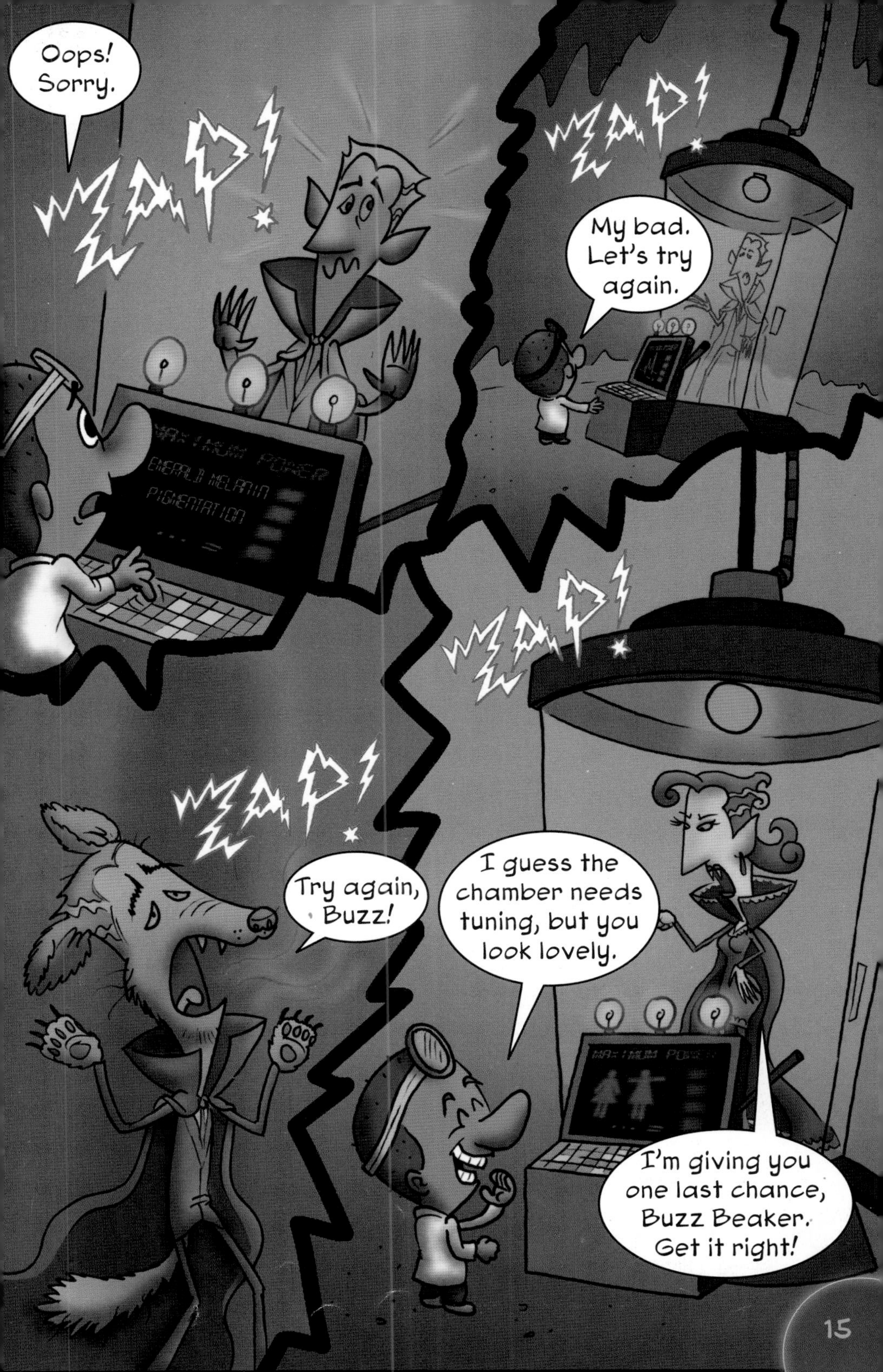
Oops! Sorry.
ZAP!
MAXIMUM POWER
EMERALD MELANIN
PIGMENTATION
ZAP!
My bad. Let's try again.
ZAP!
Try again, Buzz!
ZAP!
I guess the chamber needs tuning, but you look lovely.
MAXIMUM POWER
I'm giving you one last chance, Buzz Beaker. Get it right!

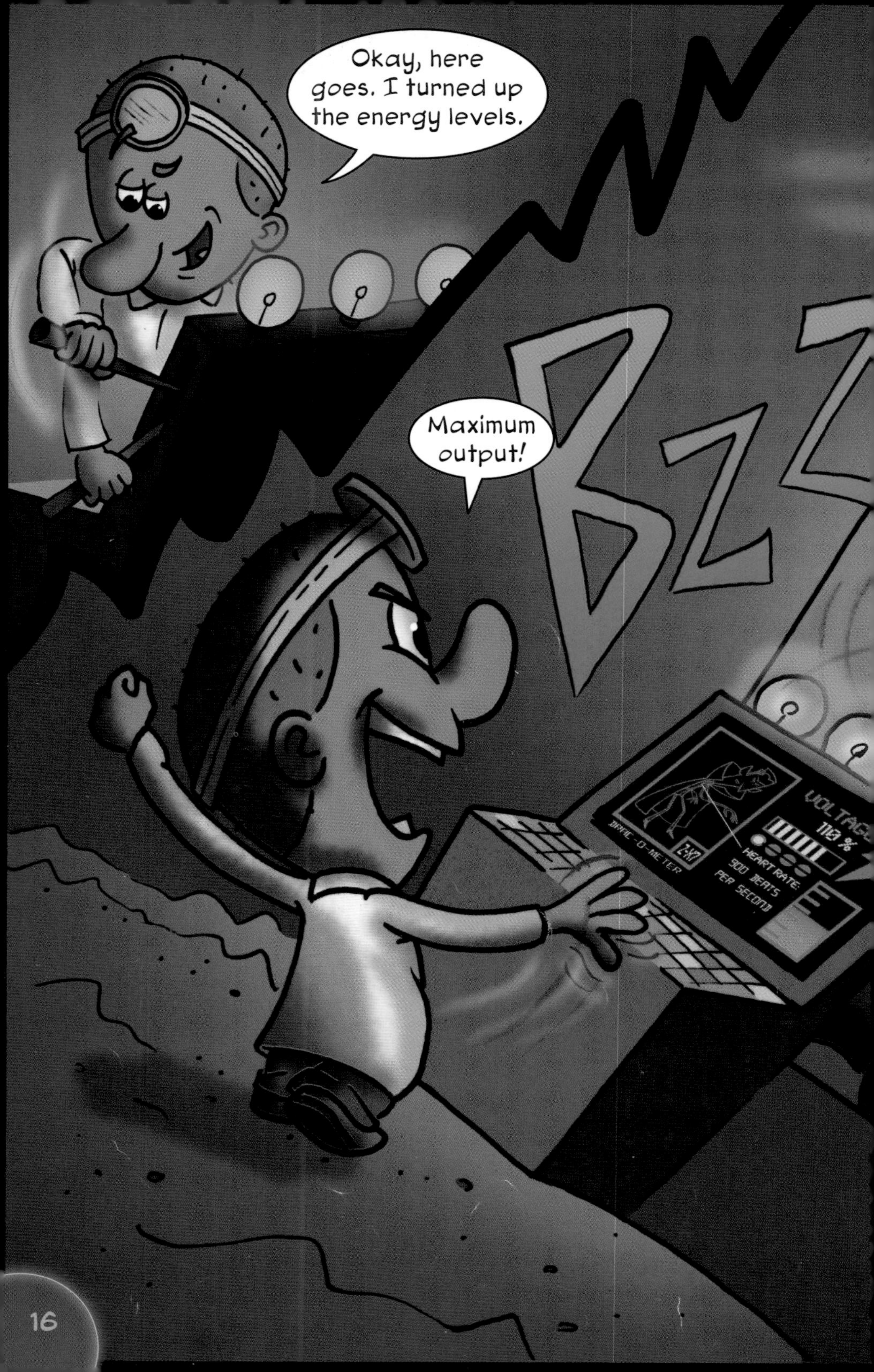
Okay, here goes. I turned up the energy levels.
Maximum output!
BZZ
VOLTAGE
110 %
HEART RATE:
500 BEATS PER SECOND
BRAC-O-METER

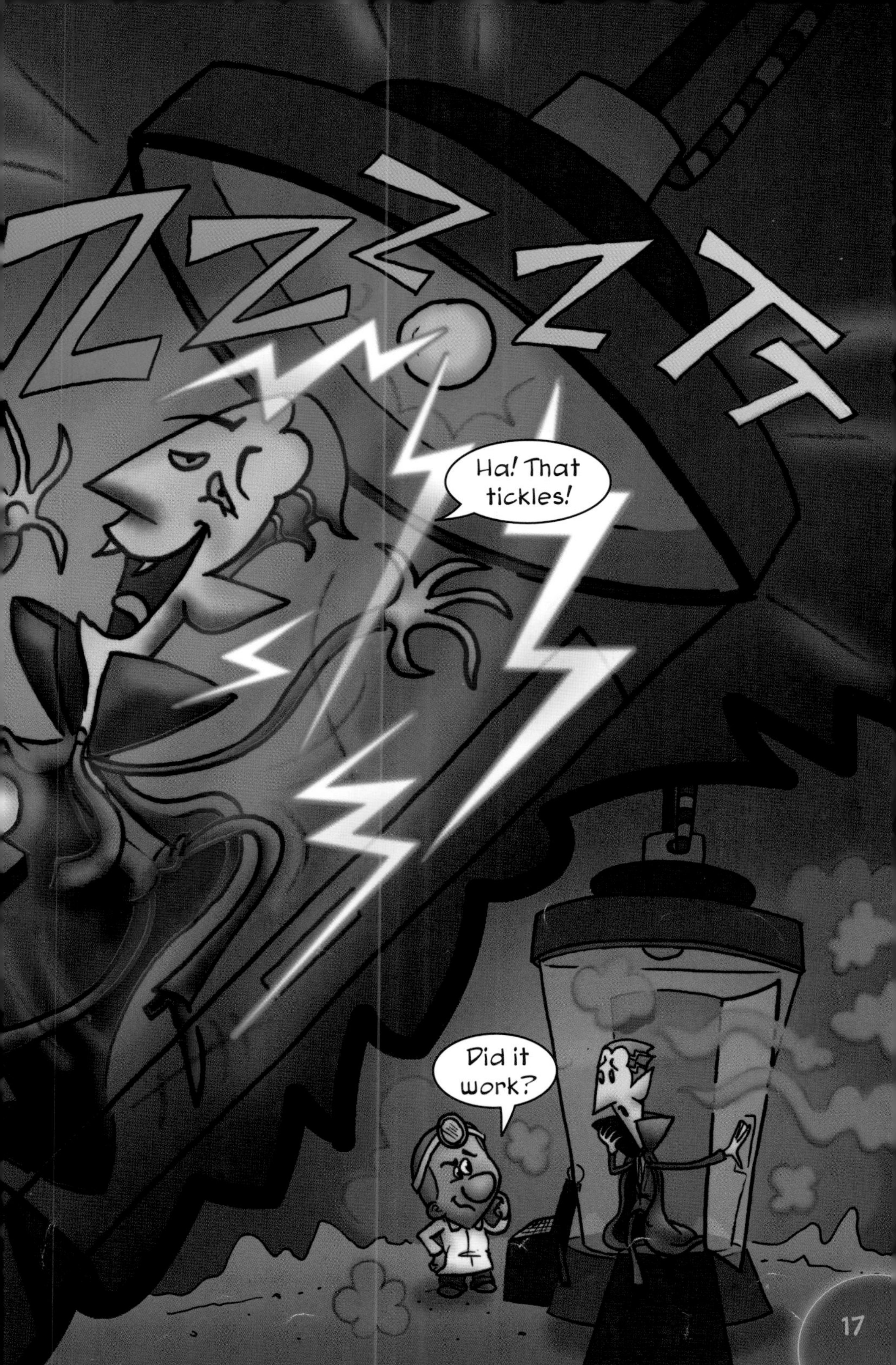
ZZZZZOTT
Ha! That tickles!
Did it work?

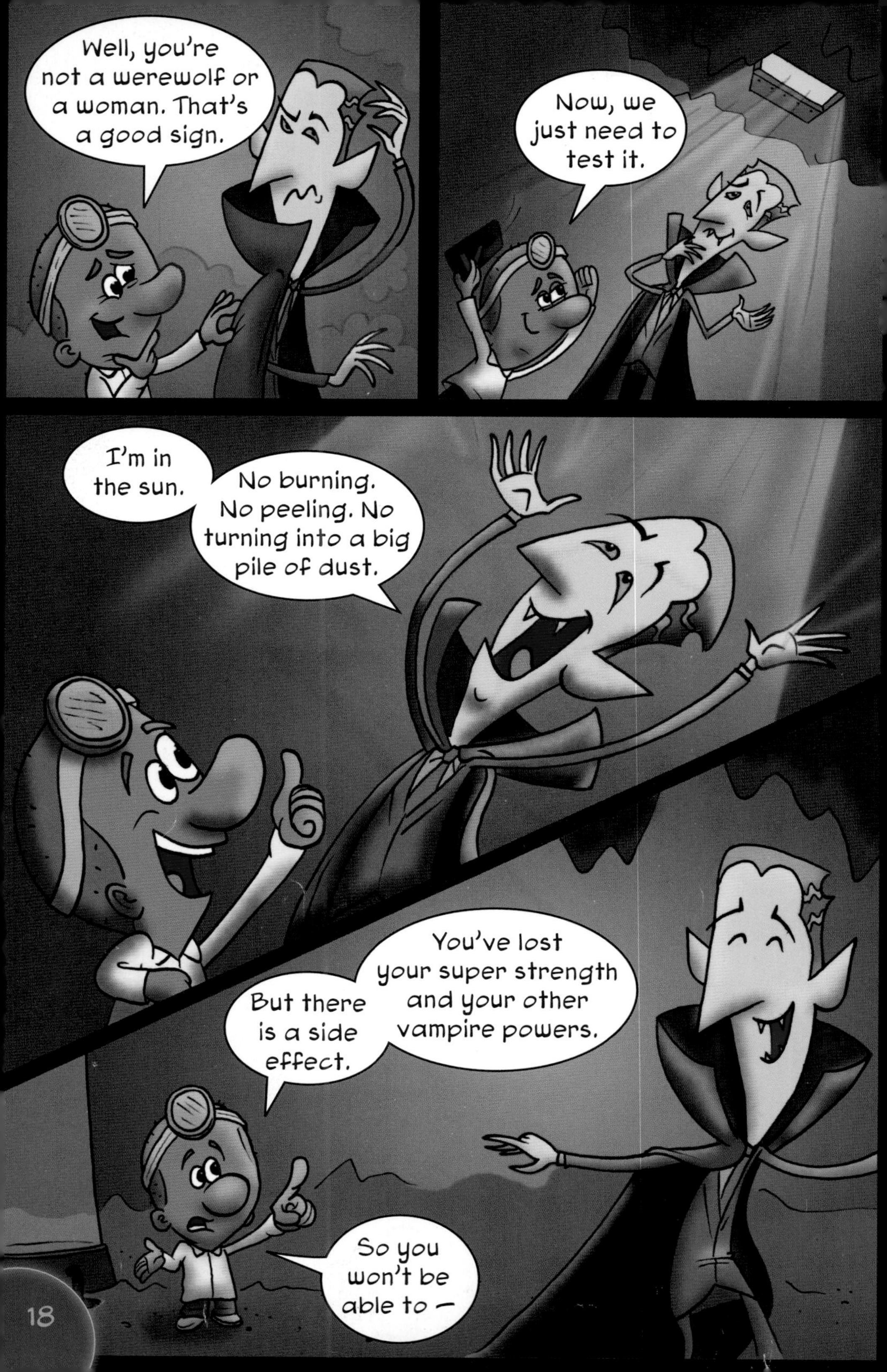
Well, you're not a werewolf or a woman. That's a good sign.
Now, we just need to test it.
I'm in the sun.
No burning. No peeling. No turning into a big pile of dust.
You've lost your super strength and your other vampire powers.
But there is a side effect.
So you won't be able to —

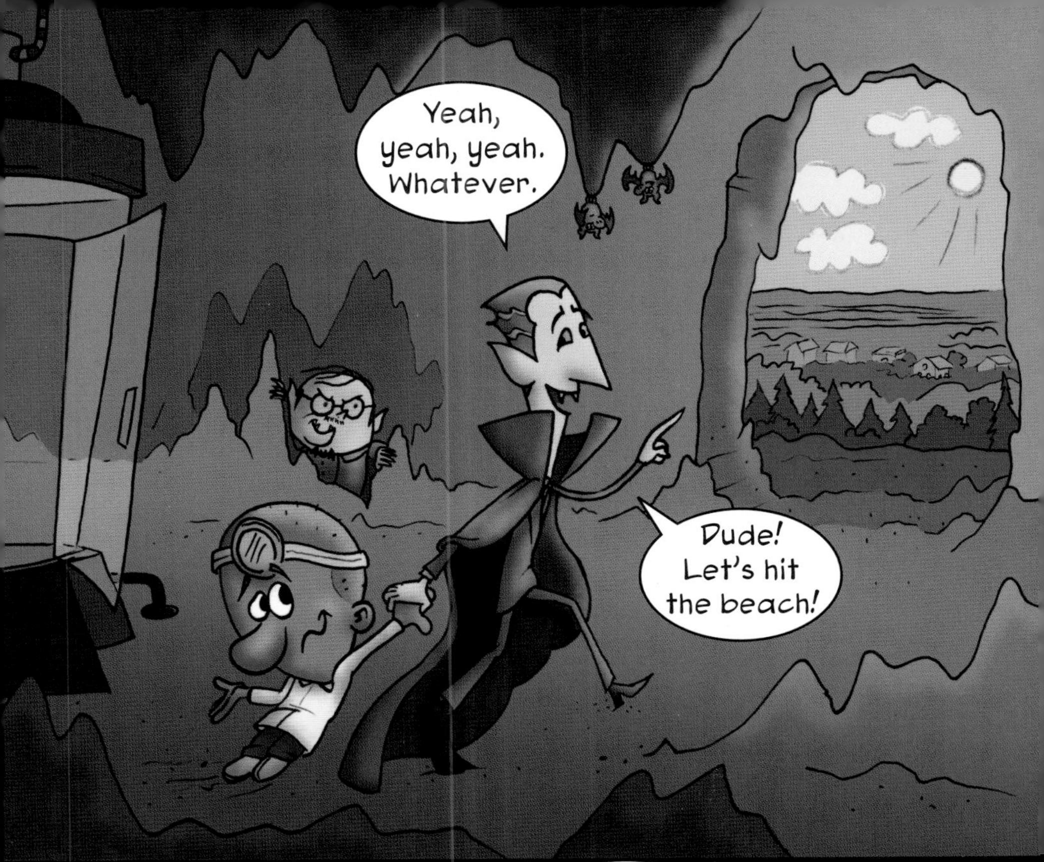
Yeah, yeah, yeah. Whatever.
Dude! Let's hit the beach!

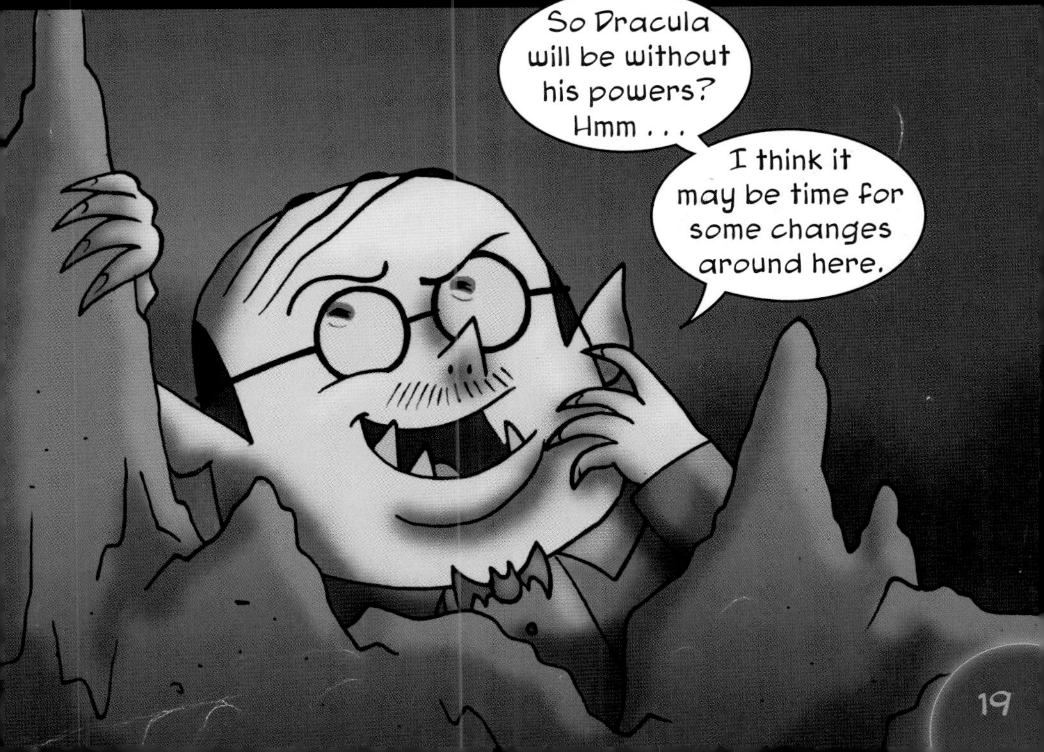
So Dracula will be without his powers? Hmm . . .
I think it may be time for some changes around here.

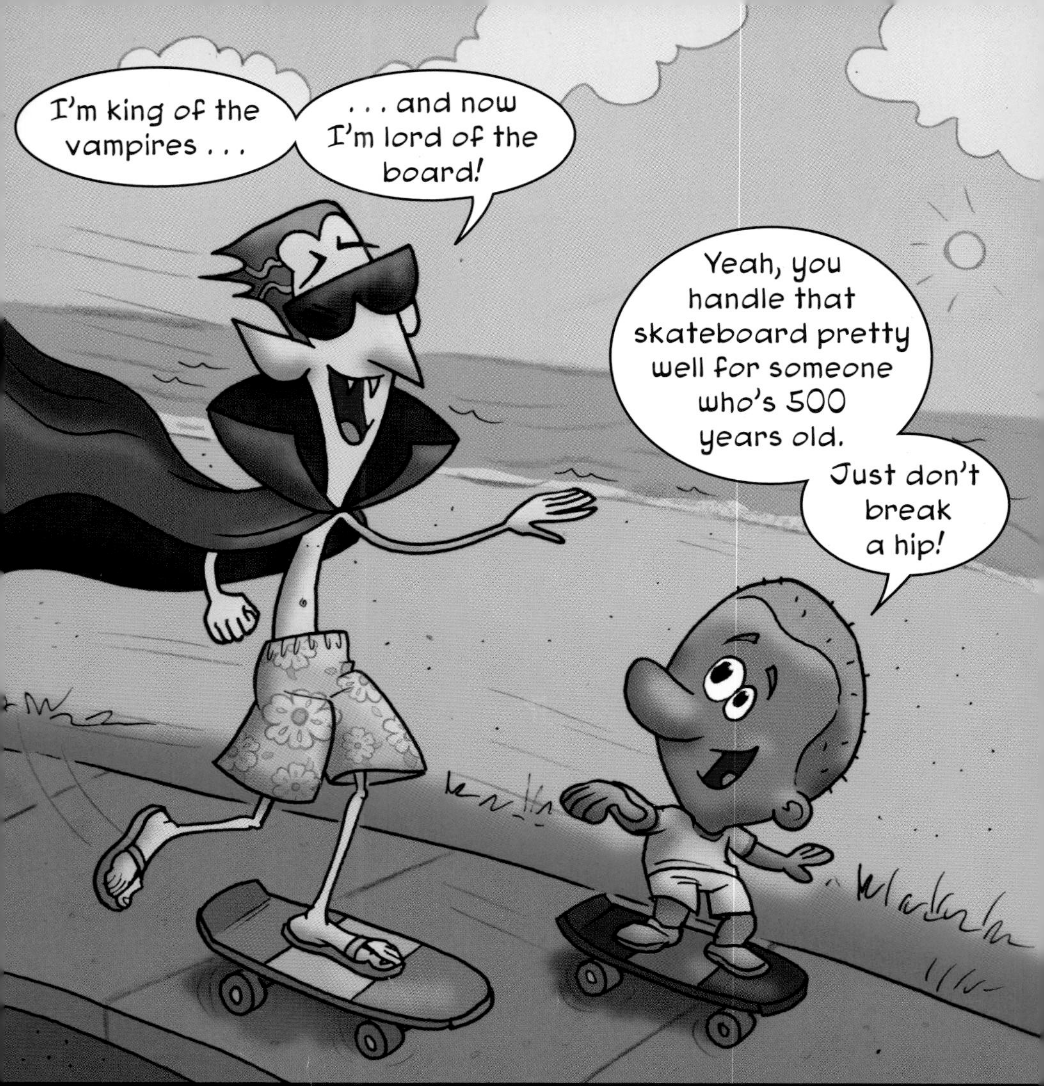
I'm king of the vampires . . .
. . . and now I'm lord of the board!
Yeah, you handle that skateboard pretty well for someone who's 500 years old.
Just don't break a hip!

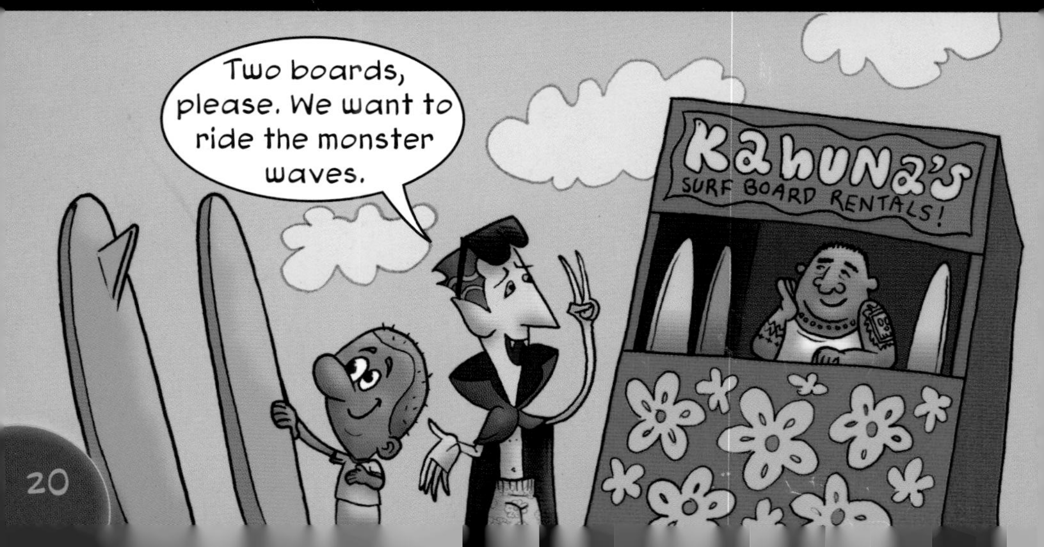
Two boards, please. We want to ride the monster waves.
Kahuna's SURF BOARD RENTALS!

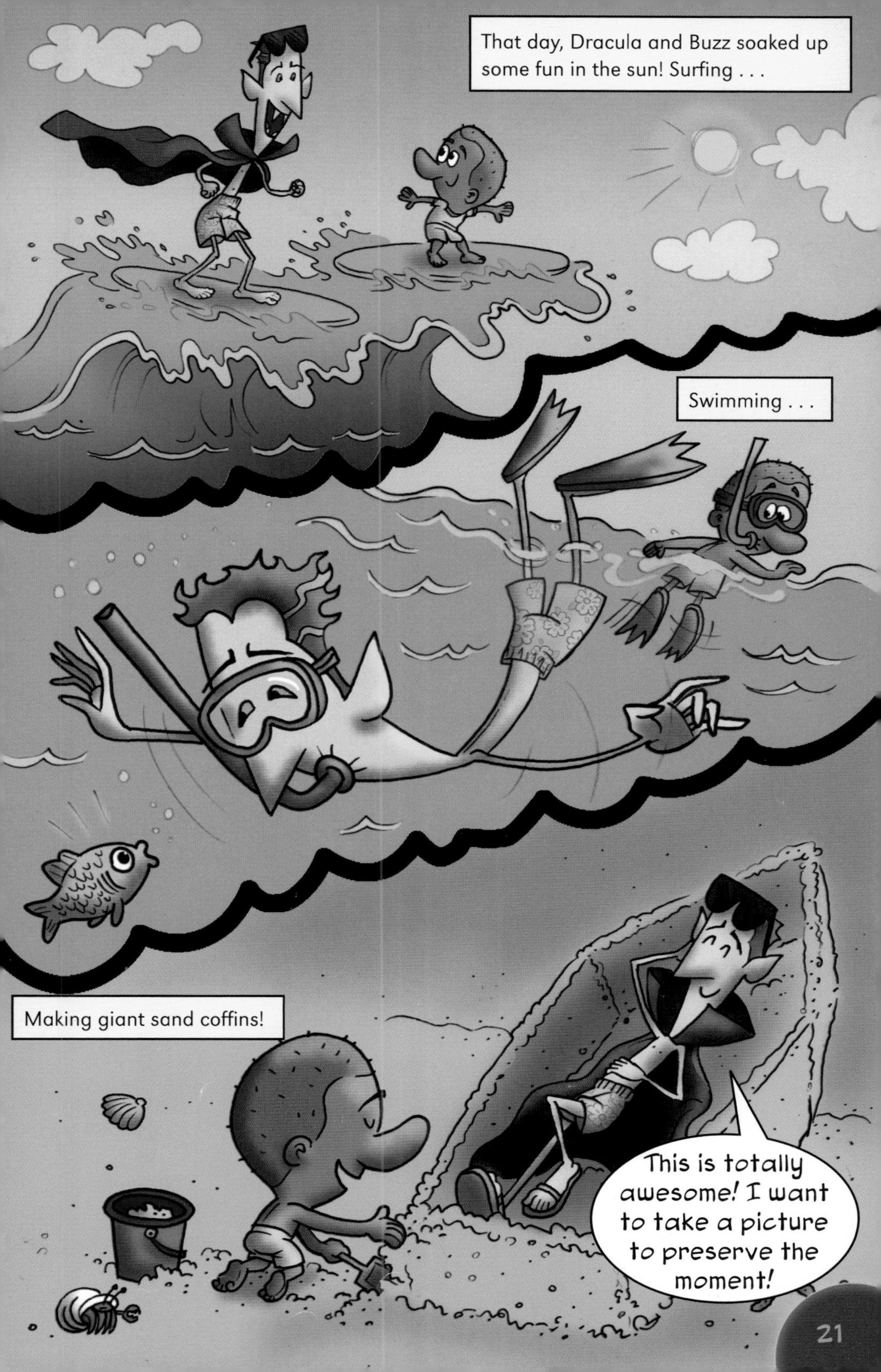
That day, Dracula and Buzz soaked up some fun in the sun! Surfing . . .
Swimming . . .
Making giant sand coffins!
This is totally awesome! I want to take a picture to preserve the moment!

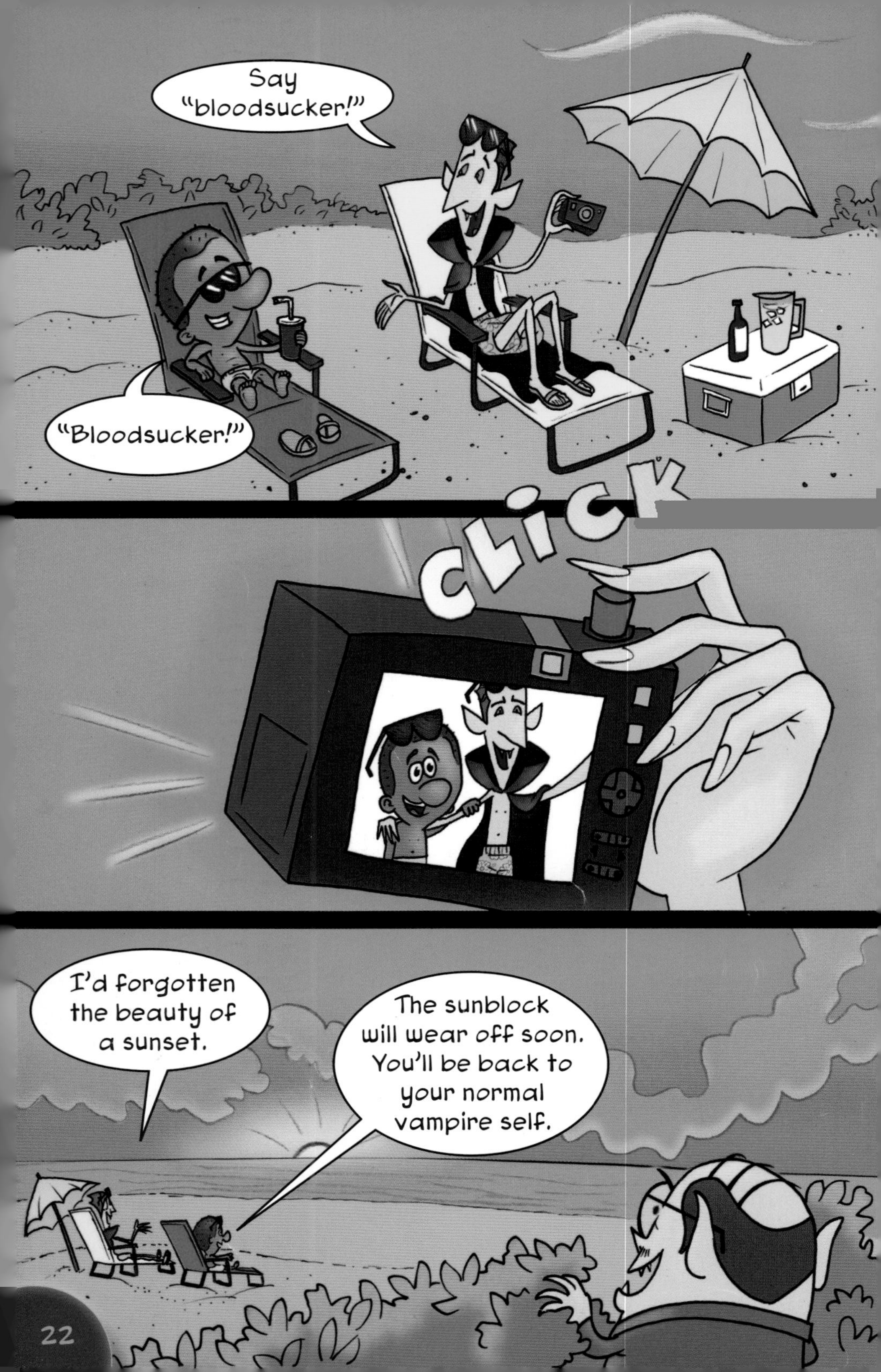
Say "bloodsucker!"
"Bloodsucker!"
CLICK
I'd forgotten the beauty of a sunset.
The sunblock will wear off soon. You'll be back to your normal vampire self.

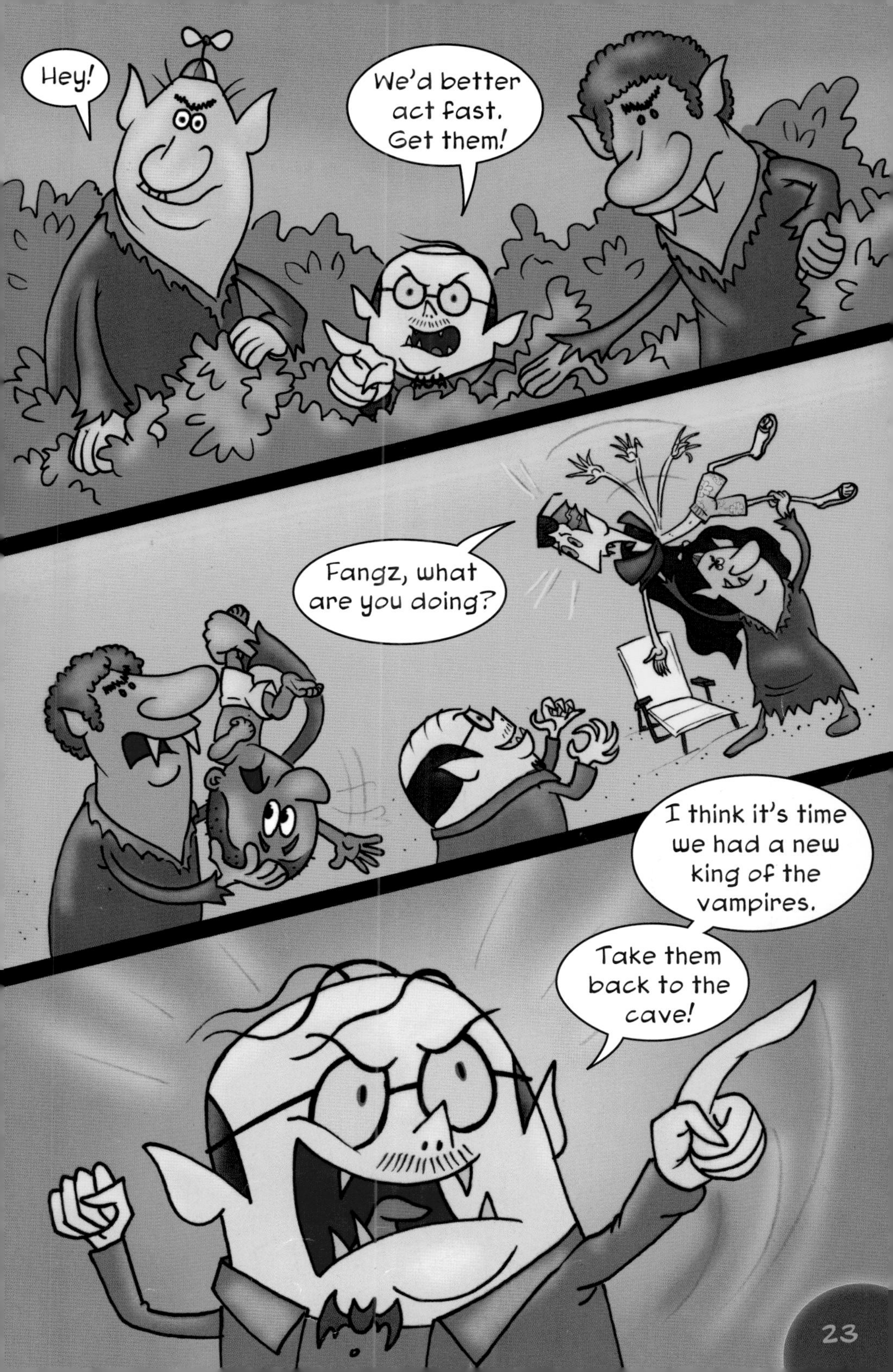
Hey!
We'd better act fast. Get them!
Fangz, what are you doing?
I think it's time we had a new king of the vampires.
Take them back to the cave!

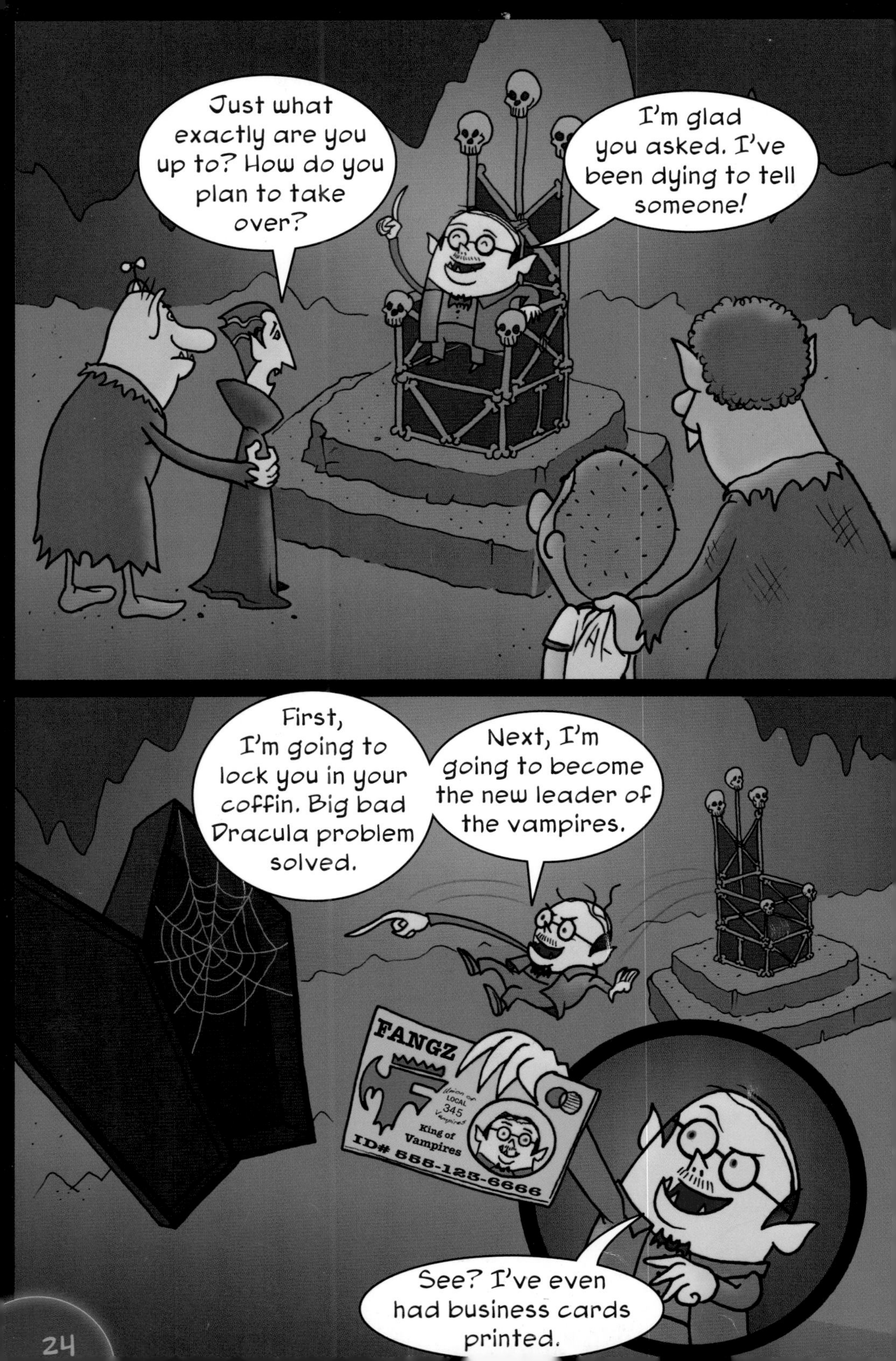
Just what exactly are you up to? How do you plan to take over?
I'm glad you asked. I've been dying to tell someone!
First, I'm going to lock you in your coffin. Big bad Dracula problem solved.
Next, I'm going to become the new leader of the vampires.
FANGZ
Union of LOCAL 345 Vampires
King of Vampires
ID# 555-123-6666
See? I've even had business cards printed.

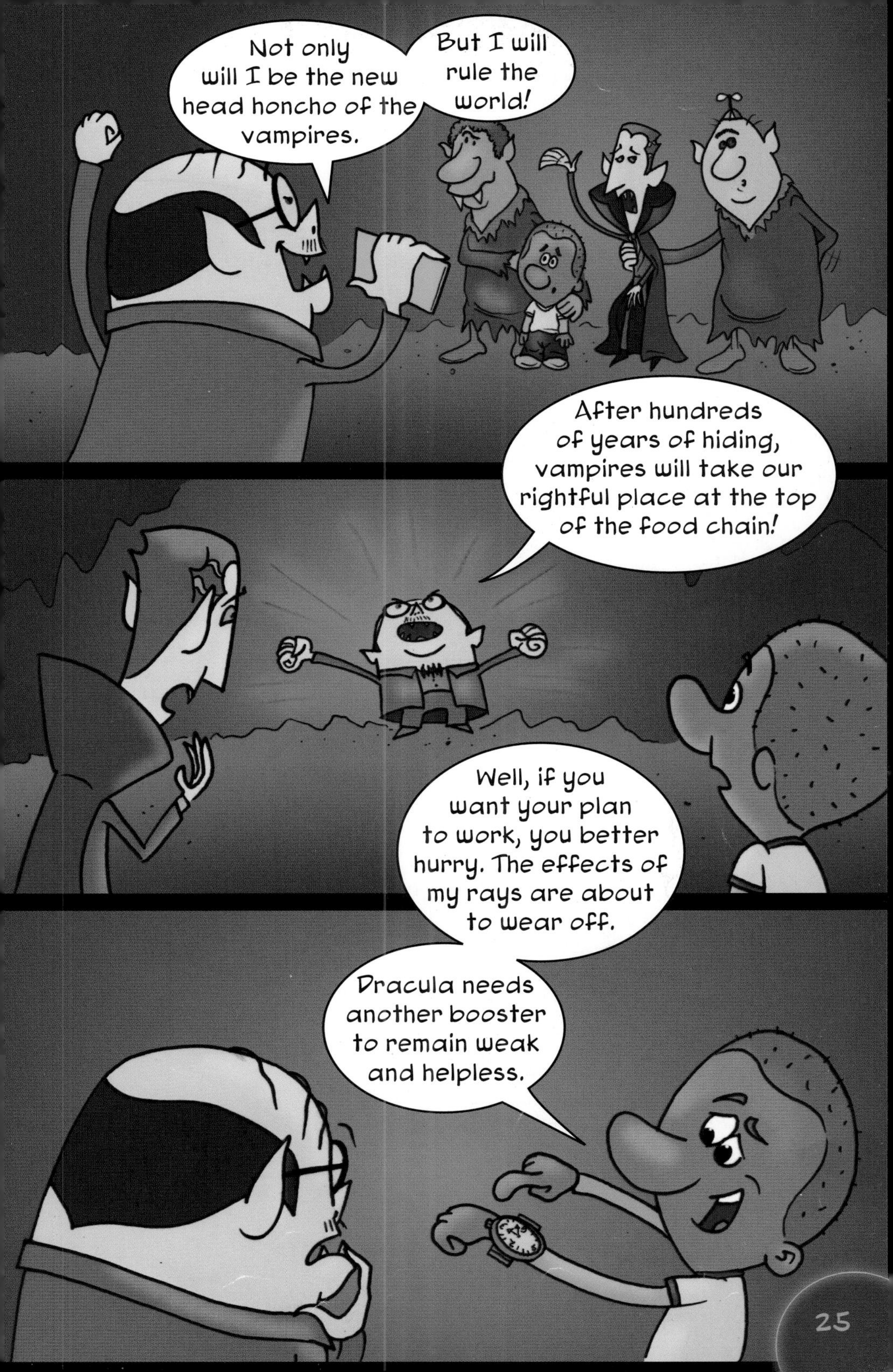
Not only will I be the new head honcho of the vampires.
But I will rule the world!
After hundreds of years of hiding, vampires will take our rightful place at the top of the food chain!
Well, if you want your plan to work, you better hurry. The effects of my rays are about to wear off.
Dracula needs another booster to remain weak and helpless.

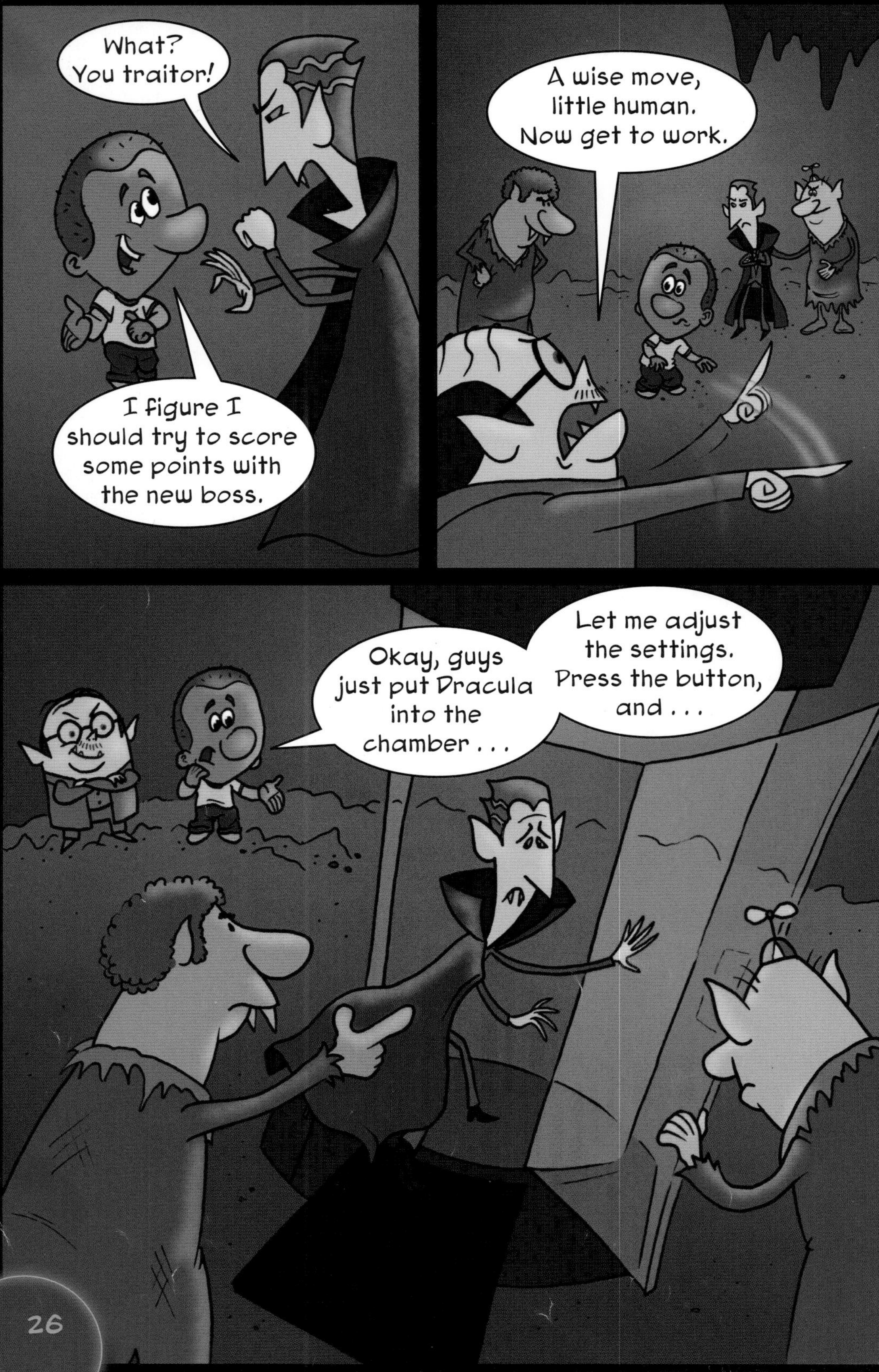
What? You traitor!
I figure I should try to score some points with the new boss.
A wise move, little human. Now get to work.
Okay, guys just put Dracula into the chamber . . .
Let me adjust the settings. Press the button, and . . .

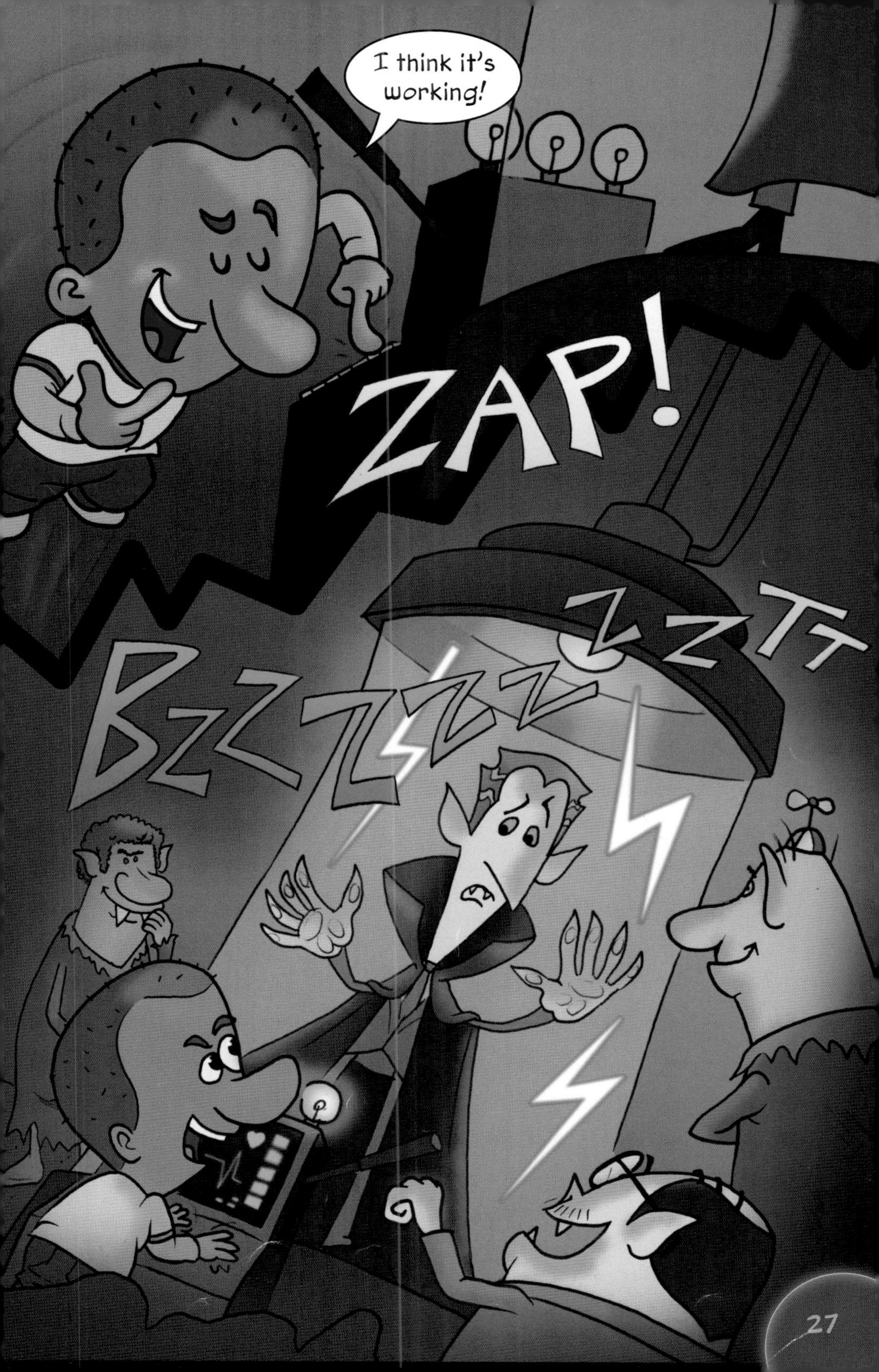
I think it's working!
ZAP!
BZZZZZZZTT

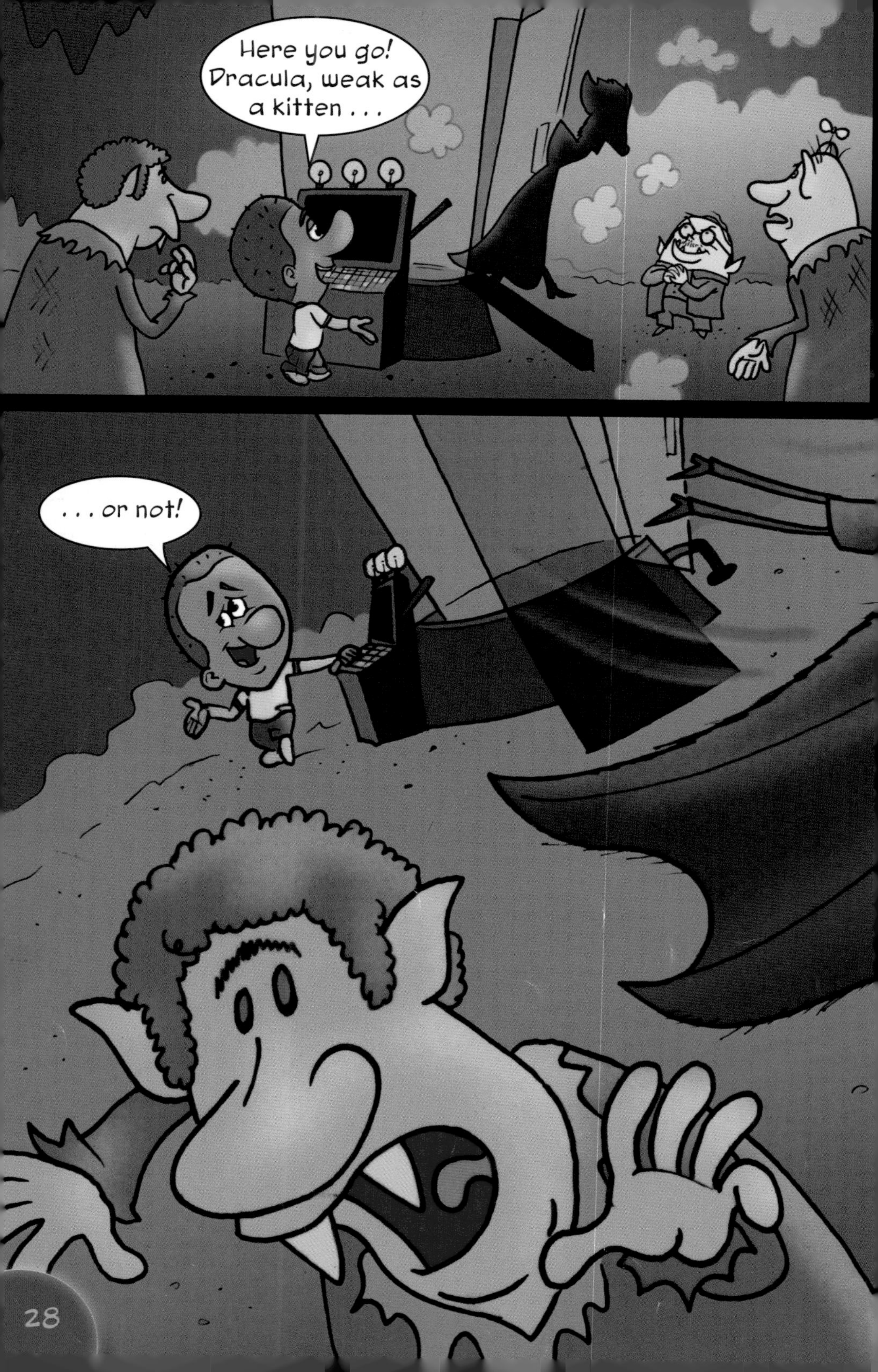
Here you go! Dracula, weak as a kitten . . .
. . . or not!

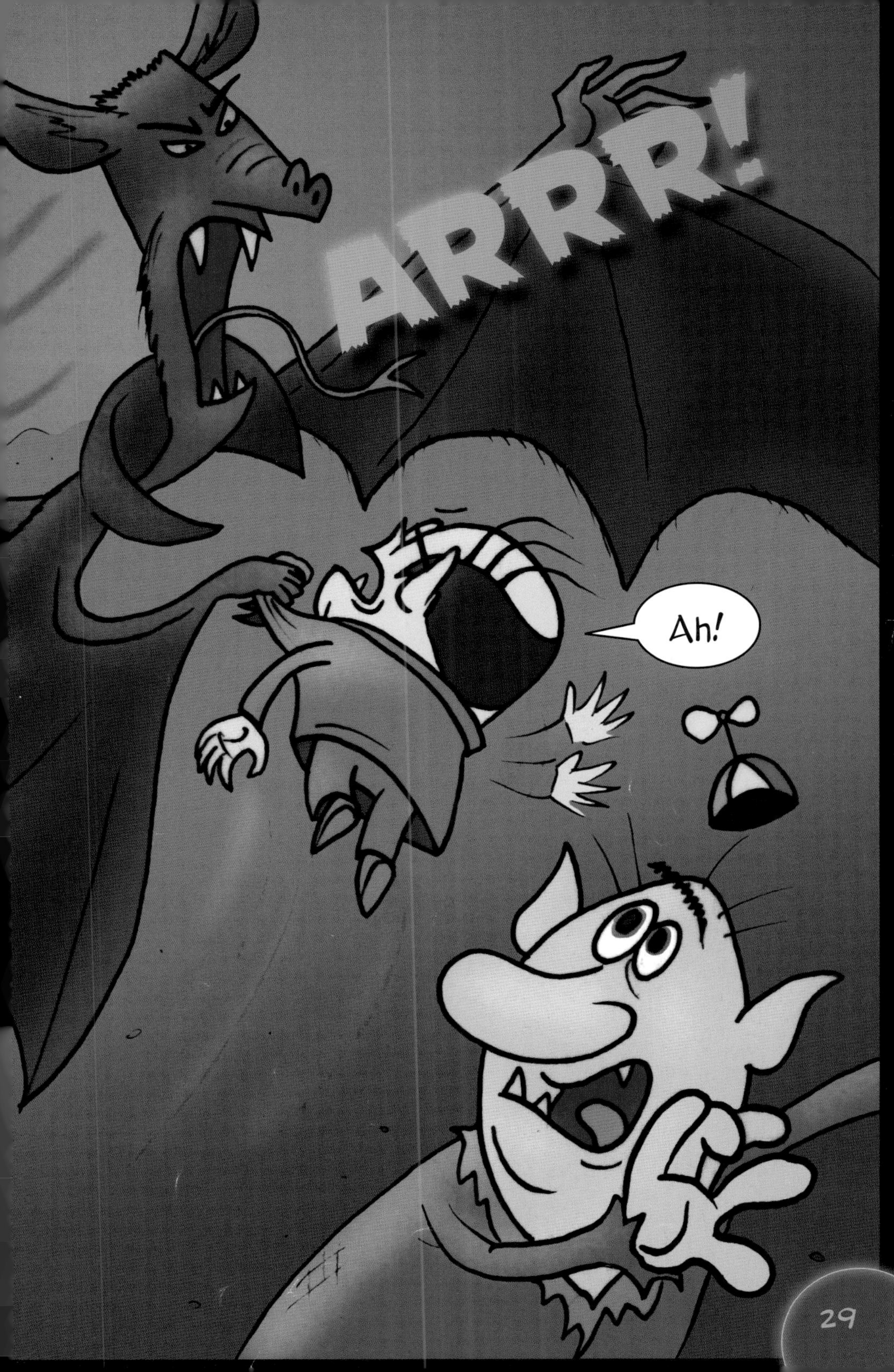
ARRR!
Ah!

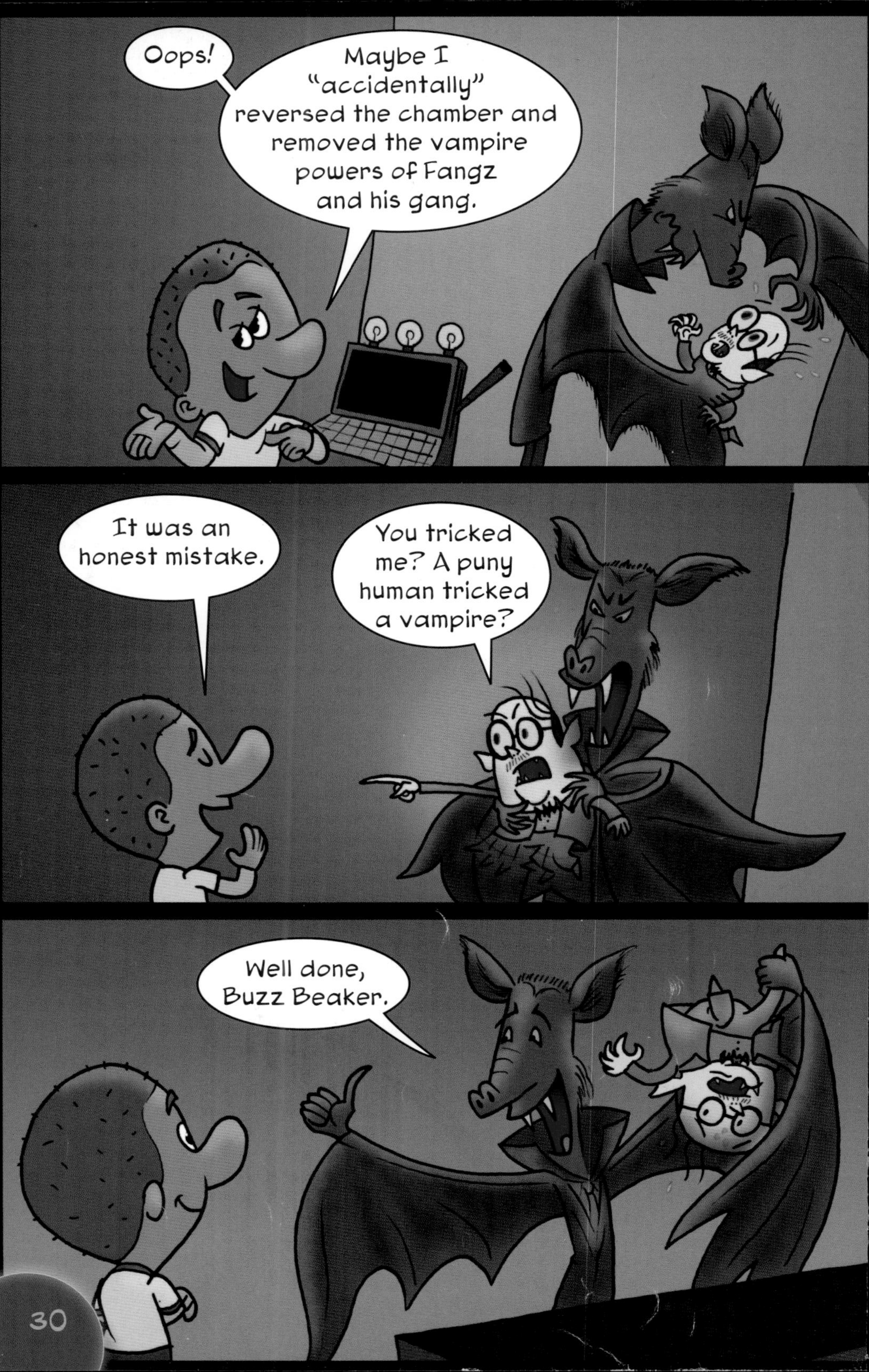

Oops!
Maybe I "accidentally" reversed the chamber and removed the vampire powers of Fangz and his gang.
It was an honest mistake.
You tricked me? A puny human tricked a vampire?
Well done, Buzz Beaker.

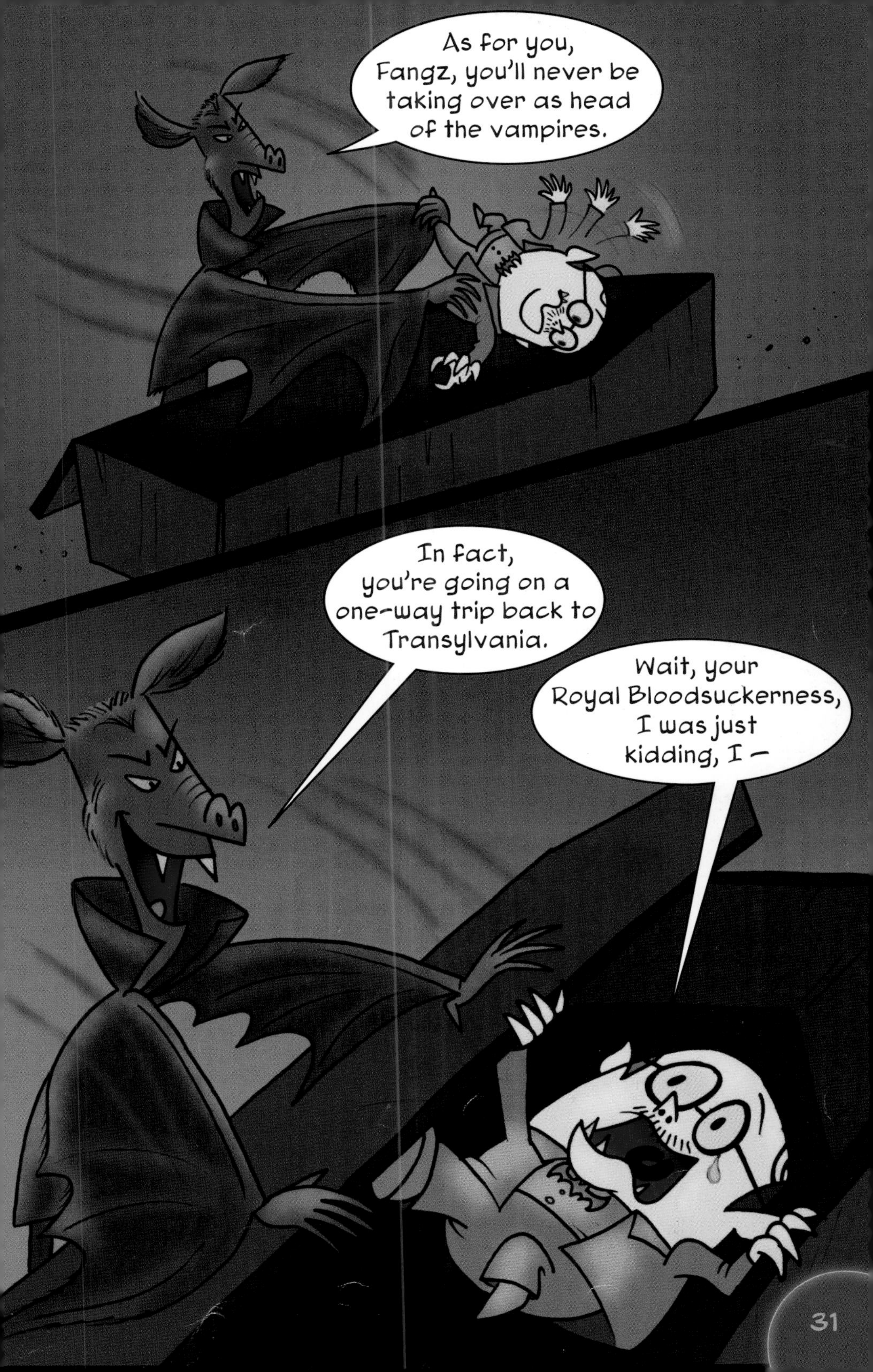
As for you, Fangz, you'll never be taking over as head of the vampires.
In fact, you're going on a one-way trip back to Transylvania.
Wait, your Royal Bloodsuckerness, I was just kidding, I —

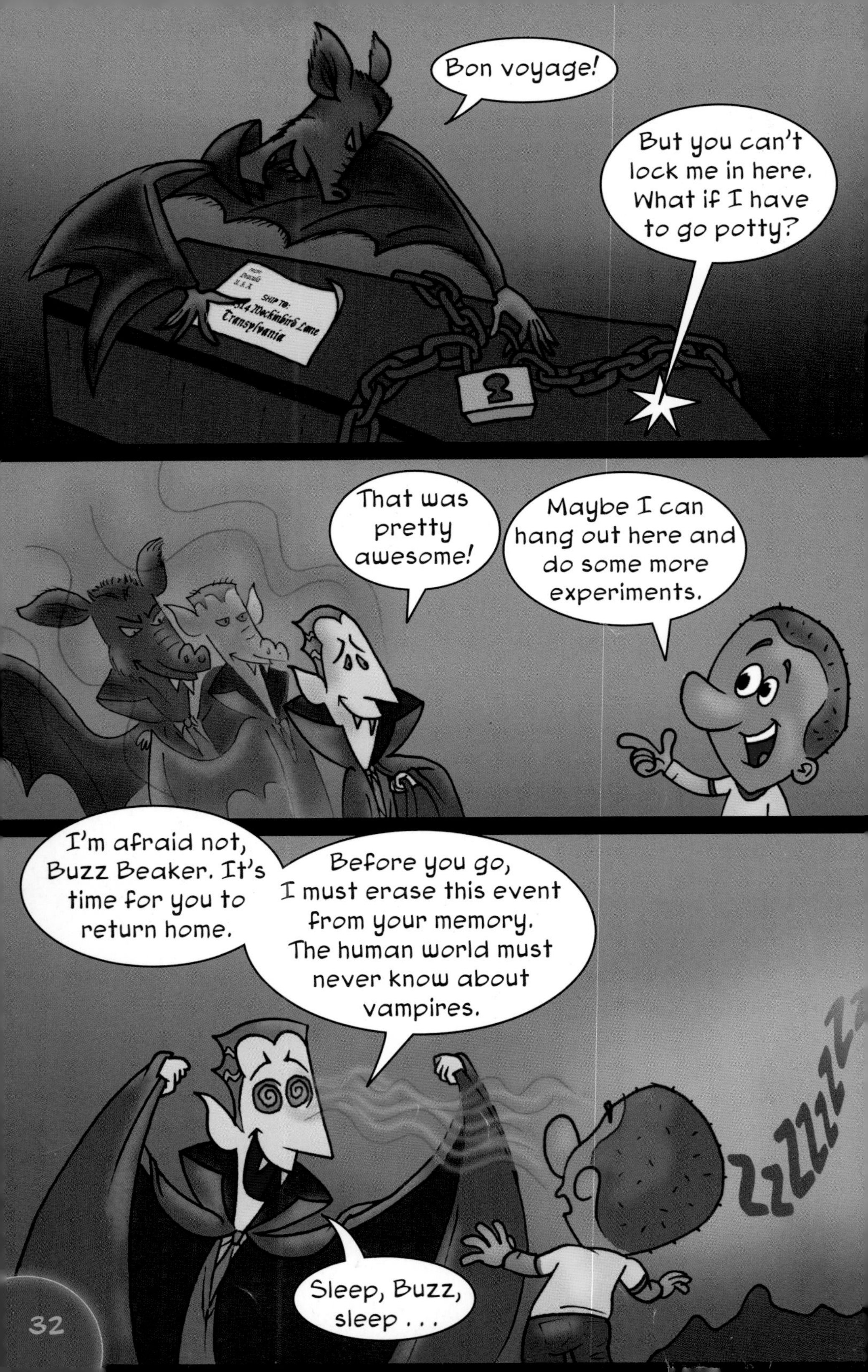
Bon voyage!
But you can't lock me in here. What if I have to go potty?
SHIP TO:
Transylvania
That was pretty awesome!
Maybe I can hang out here and do some more experiments.
I'm afraid not, Buzz Beaker. It's time for you to return home.
Before you go, I must erase this event from your memory. The human world must never know about vampires.
Sleep, Buzz, sleep . . .
ZzZZzzZZz

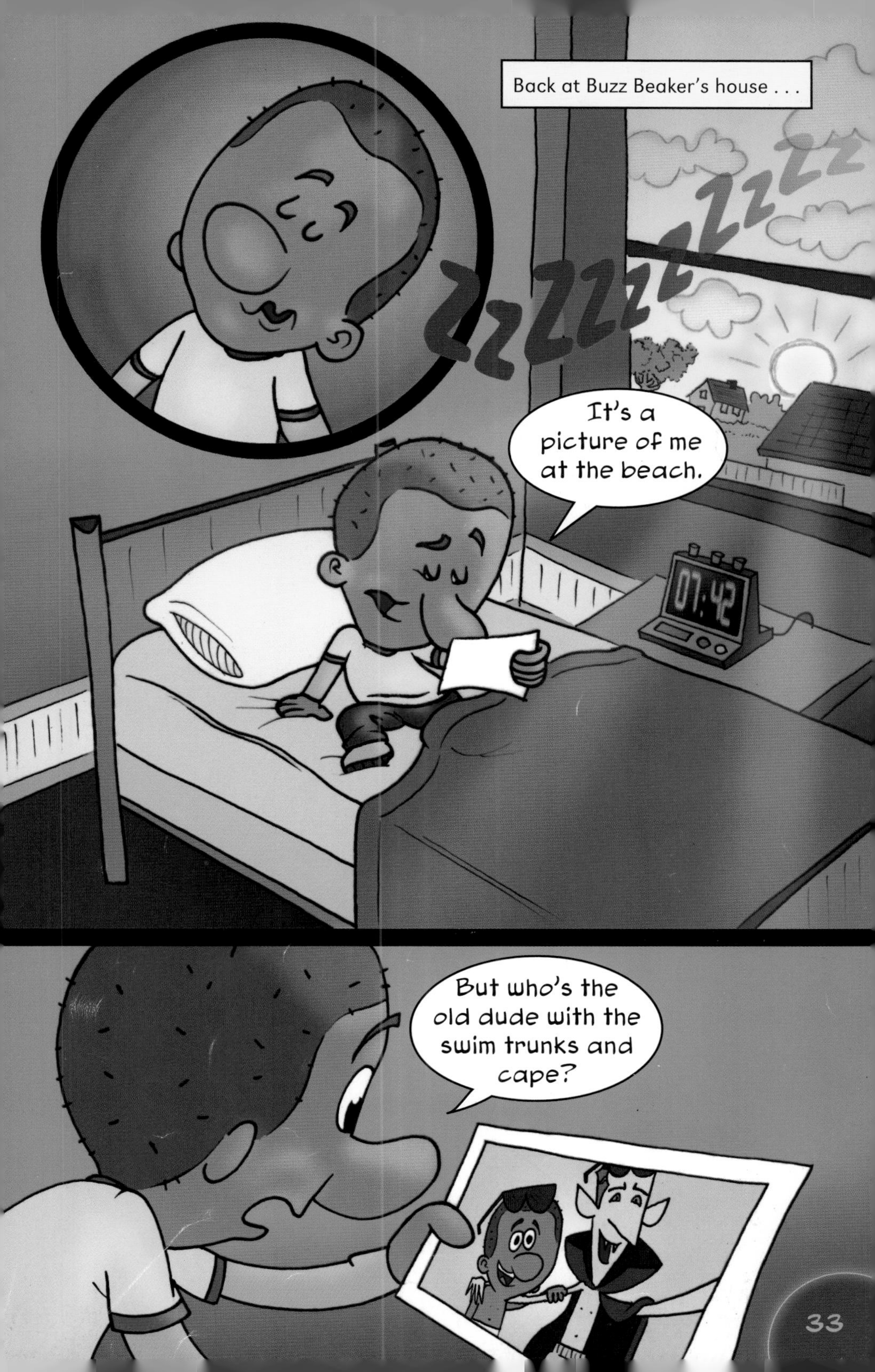
Back at Buzz Beaker's house . . .
ZzZzzzzzzzz
It's a picture of me at the beach.
07:42
But who's the old dude with the swim trunks and cape?

About the Author

Born in 1962 in Denver, Colorado, Scott Nickel works by day at Paws, Inc., Jim Davis's famous Garfield studio, and he freelances by night. Burning the midnight oil, Scott has created hundreds of humorous greeting cards and written several children's books, short fiction for *Boys' Life* magazine, comic strips, and lots of really funny knock-knock jokes. He was raised in southern California, but in 1995 Scott moved to Indiana, where he currently lives with his wife, two sons, six cats, and several sea monkeys.

About the Illustrator

Andy Smith knew he wanted to be an illustrator (if he couldn't be a space adventurer, superhero, or ghost hunter). After graduating from college in 1998, he began working at a handful of New York City animation studios on shows like *Courage the Cowardly Dog* and *Sheep in the Big City.* Since then, he has worked as a character designer, freelance illustrator, and taught high school and college art classes. Andy lives in Ipswich, Massachusetts, with his wife, Karen.

Glossary

booster (BOO-stur)—given to increase the effect of something

chamber (CHAYM-bur)—a large room or area

laboratory (LAB-ruh-tor-ee)—a room containing special equipment for people to use in scientific experiments

mortal (MOR-tuhl)—a human being who cannot live forever

traitor (TRAY-tur)—someone who helps the enemy

ultimate (UHL-tuh-mit)—greatest and best, or last and final

vampire (VAM-pyre)—according to myths and folktales, a vampire is a person who rises from the dead at night. Vampires feed on the blood of other people. Yuck!

More About Vampires

Vampire myths have been around for thousands of years. These myths have been found in almost all cultures around the world.

Dracula, the most well-known vampire, was created by Bram Stoker. In 1897, Bram Stoker wrote the novel *Dracula*. This novel made the vampire legend famous.

Vampires cannot die. However, they do have some weaknesses. They are afraid of crucifixes, holy water, and garlic. They can be killed by a stake through the heart, fire, and direct sunlight. Or by chopping off their head.

Vampires have extreme strength, but do not have a reflection. They often sleep upside down like bats.

In many books and movies, vampires turn into vampire bats. Vampire bats are real animals that feed on blood. However, they don't usually kill their prey. In fact, vampire bats are small, gentle animals.

Through the years, vampires have been portrayed in many different ways. They have been shown as space creatures, rock stars, friendly neighbors, criminals, and normal teenagers.

Discussion Questions

1. As a scientist, Buzz Beaker creates lots of new things. He even invents his own flavor of ice cream. If you were a scientist, what would you invent?

2. At first Fangz is a helpful sidekick to Dracula. Then he turns into a traitor. How do you think Dracula felt when Fangz betrayed him? Have you ever been betrayed?

3. At the end of the story, Dracula erases Buzz's memory. Why do you think he did that?

Writing Prompts

1. Dracula lives in a secret cave. If you were a monster, describe where you would live and why.

2. When Dracula wants to go in the sun, Buzz creates a sunblock chamber. Describe what you would do to help Dracula in his quest to enjoy the sunlight.

3. At the end of the story, Fangz is sent to Transylvania. What would you have done to punish him?

Internet Sites

The book may be over, but the adventure is just beginning.

Do you want to read more about the subjects or ideas in this book? Want to play cool games or watch videos about the authors who write these books? Then go to FactHound. At *www.facthound.com*, you'll be able to do all that, and more. The FactHound website can also send you to other safe Internet sites.

Check it out!